No One Said a Word

Fiction by Paula Varasavsky

El resto de su vida

Nadie alzaba la voz

No One Said a Word

No One Said
a Word

Paula Varsavsky

Translated from the Spanish by
Anne McLean

WingsPress

San Antonio, Texas
2013

No One Said A Word © 2013 by Wings Press, for Paula Varsavsky.

First English language (hardback) edition published by
Ontario Review Press © 2000.
Originally published as *Nadie alzaba la voz*
© 1994 by Emecé Editores, S.A.
English language translation © 2000 by Anne McLean
All rights reserved.

Cover image, untitled collage © 2011 by Silvia Flichman
www.silviaflichman.com.ar/

First Wings Press Edition

Paperback Edition ISBN: 978-1-60940-269-3
Epub ISBN: 978-1-60940-270-9
Kindle ISBN: 978-1-60940-271-6
Library PDF ISBN: 978-1-60940-272-3

Wings Press
627 E. Guenther
San Antonio, Texas 78210
Phone/fax: (210) 271-7805
On-line catalogue and ordering:www.wingspress.com
All Wings Press titles are distributed to the trade by
Independent Publishers Group
www.ipgbook.com

Library of Congress Cataloging-in-Publication Data

Varsavsky, Paula, 1963-
[Nadie alzaba la voz. English]
No one said a word / Paula Varsavsky ; translated from the Spanish by
Anne McLean.—1st pbk ed.
p. cm.
ISBN 978-1-60940-269-3 (pbk : alk. paper) -- ISBN 978-1-60940-
270-9 (ePub eBook) -- ISBN 978-1-60940-271-6 (Kindle eBook) -- ISBN
978-1-60940-272-3 (library pdf eBook)
I. McLean, Anne, 1962- II. Title.
PQ7798.32.A76 N313 2013
863'.64

For Silvia Waisman and Carlos Varsavsky,
my parents

No One Said a Word

Dad phoned from New York. He told me he'd be coming to Buenos Aires. It didn't cheer me up like other times. Dad said, "It's not for pleasure, this trip. My brother's having heart surgery. We don't want your grandmother to find out. When he gets in to Buenos Aires from Bogotá he'll let you know which hotel he's staying in. And you can tell me."

I felt anxious when I hung up. Dad sounded really worried. I felt sorry for him. For the first time ever I felt sorry for Dad. The thought of going through such a tough time with his brother seemed to weigh him down. Dad's wife wasn't coming with him. I was the only one in Buenos Aires who knew. I was overwhelmed. It was too much responsibility to support Dad through something like this. His brother in Bogotá was the only one he had left alive.

As the days went by, my unease increased. I talked to Juan. I told him what was going on in my family. He asked me if I was afraid my uncle would die. I said no. I was scared for Dad.

· · ·

My university entrance exam was coming up. I couldn't study. I thought maybe Dad could help me. I changed my mind. I'd rather study alone. It would have been better if I could've taken the exam before they operated on my uncle. But no. The date for the surgery was already set. My entrance exam didn't matter to anyone.

The day before Dad was to arrive, the situation became unbearable. I had to leave class because I couldn't stand it one minute longer. There'd been several heart attacks in my family. My Dad's father and his older brother both died fairly young of heart attacks. I was so upset that evening, I called my therapist. She'd been off work for two months: she was expecting a baby. She listened to me and asked me to calm down. Tomorrow, she told me, I'd see Dad and could tell him how much I loved him and that I was worried about him. And in any case, she added that if I was still worried after seeing Dad, to call her back. When I hung up, my anxiety remained intact.

I wondered what would happen if Dad died. Immediately I tried to erase that thought. When I was already in bed, still awake, the telephone rang: it was Dad. He told me he was still in New York: the plane was delayed. He might miss his connection in Río, and that had him practically in shock. He'd travelled so often and never missed a flight! We were dealing with a real blot on his existence here. I told him if he missed his plane it didn't matter; I'd go to the airport anyway, and wait for him there. He asked me not to; if he missed his connection in Río he'd call me.

Dad didn't call. Part of the ritual of his visits involved me going out to Ezeiza airport to meet him. I knew he liked to be met. I liked going. As usual, the taxi came to pick me up. Mom came downstairs with me and told me to take care. In the car I heard that song that goes, "He's alright, my old man...."

When I got to Ezeiza I found out the plane from Río was delayed. I was glad. I spoke to Ana on the phone from Ezeiza. I told her Dad was probably just about to arrive since he hadn't called. I was studying Logic for the Mathematics entrance exam. I was pleased to be able to prove the validity of logic to every-day life: if P denotes the premise "Dad missed his connection in Río" and Q "He would call me," the rule of inference—if P then Q; if not P therefore not Q—applied perfectly. I thought, "If Dad missed his connection in Río, he would have called me; he didn't call, therefore he hadn't missed his connection in Río." How cool, *Modus Tollens* worked in real life! I informed Ana of my brilliant deduction.

When they announced the arrival of Dad's plane, I hurried over to the customs exit. I saw the first passengers come out: huge hugs from their friends and relatives. I watched these affectionate receptions rather enviously. I thought how Dad and I were always quite restrained in our greetings. But this time I felt like hugging him. The hugs and kisses all around me continued, along with a few tears. I kept looking. I was anxiously waiting for Dad to appear. At the same time I was enviously watching the big families. Those where all of them go together to the airport to pick up the one who's arriving; those where they all live in the same city; those where there's a mom and a dad who love each other. All those things I never had. "They're almost all out," I heard someone say. But my dad wasn't there.

I called home. Ester told me that Dad was still in Brazil and was trying to get in touch with me, to come home quickly. He'd already phoned several times. I didn't go home. I got a taxi, went to the university. I felt, all of a sudden, that I couldn't miss the last classes. The entrance exam was the following week. I spoke to Ester again from school. She insisted I come back there immediately. I had the feeling that something really serious was going on. I didn't go to class. I went home.

From the hallway I heard the phone ringing. Ester opened the door and told me to answer it. "I'm sure it's your dad." I heard my brother Luis's voice. He lived in New York too. He told me that the worst possible thing had happened. He asked if Mom was there. No. Mom wasn't home. Then Luis said he wouldn't tell me. I insisted. I told him that anyway, Ester was right there beside me. He told me to ask Ester to hold my hand and that Dad had died. I screamed and burst into tears. My vision clouded over. I threw down the receiver. I couldn't believe it, I didn't want to believe it, I wanted to go back in time. For the world to stop. I went and locked myself in my room. I called Ana. She was in the middle of her bachelorette party; she'd come straight over. I called Laura. I said the same thing to everyone: "My dad died." That was the only thing I could say, and then I'd start crying again. I called Juan. Then Raúl. Raúl wasn't home. The first to arrive was Ana. Then Laura came. She hugged me and we both started to cry. At that moment Mom came home. I heard Ester tell her, "Señor Manuel died." "Señor Manuel who?" asked Mom. I don't remember what Ester answered. But

I can imagine. Mom couldn't believe it. Me neither. I felt the need to tell lots of people. Each time I said it, it still struck me as incredible. I couldn't stop repeating it to myself: Dad died, Dad died. The telephone rang every little while. It was Luis. He wanted me to go there. One of the times he called I asked how it happened. Where it happened. Dad had died on the airplane, he had a heart attack. It was a silent death. The stewardess told how Dad had come up to ask her for a glass of water. That he'd told her he wasn't feeling well. And then he died. Yes, he died. Without another word.

My head was swimming. I didn't know where I'd find the strength to take a flight to New York. To go to Daddy's funeral. Nevertheless, it was imperative that I go. I had to be there. Take a plane by myself. Travel all night. No, I didn't want to go. "I don't want Dad to die."

I called Mara. I told her that Dad had died and she came straight over. Two of my brother's best friends came over. Raúl came. Mara despised him, and this time she didn't hide it. Raúl and I had broken up eight months ago. Knowing it would bother Raúl, Mara asked me about a guy I liked at school.

Some relatives came over in the evening. I didn't even want to see them. Laura and Mara stayed. The three of us were in the kitchen and Mom came in. I didn't want to see her either. At that moment I wanted another mom. A mom who'd loved Dad. I knew my mom hated him. She'd always spoken badly of him. Everything Dad did was awful, even dying. But now she was screwed. Now Dad was mine forever and she was nobody.

Laura left. Mara stayed over. I couldn't get to sleep all night. Nor did I have anything to say. A deep, sharp pain settled into me. It all seemed like a movie. I couldn't believe it was true. I wanted someone to come and tell me it wasn't, that it was all a misunderstanding. No one did.

Luis phoned: he'd reserved a ticket for the next day. A problem arose: my passport had expired. It would be impossible to renew it in one day. I spoke to Dad's secretary in New York. She told me not to worry about that. They'd arrange everything. I'd definitely be able to travel the next day.

Mom offered to come with me. I didn't want her to. What was this? How would Susana, Dad's wife, feel if she saw Mom? Who was the widow? Were there two widows, or what? No, I'd rather Mom stayed in Buenos Aires. I couldn't stand the idea of her coming.

My aunt phoned, my father's brother's wife who lived in Colombia. She and her husband were now in Buenos Aires. She wanted to know what was happening, if Dad had arrived or not. They told her Dad had died. But of course, my uncle couldn't be told that his brother had just died of a heart attack before his operation. My aunt then wanted me to go and tell my grandmother. She didn't want to go. I shouted that I wasn't going to notify anyone of anything and I couldn't care less how my grandmother found out. I never understood why everyone in my family was so scared of telling my grandmother that another of her descendants had died when she was the one who stood it best.

The next day I went to the university. I explained my situation. I couldn't take the entrance exam because my dad had died. I asked them to please give me another date. There was no respite. It seemed like someone was enjoying my torment. Luckily Laura came with me. She was a real comfort.

I went back home. I was in my room. Mom came in to tell me that the police had come to renew my passport. I filled in the form, they took my fingerprints. There were two agents in civilian clothes. They carried briefcases with everything necessary to renew passports. They even had new passports. They completed the whole procedure right then.

Mom told me they'd come to the house earlier. When I was at school. It was no trouble to them to go and look for me there. They asked Mom to go with them in a green Falcon. On the way into the university, they exchanged friendly greetings with the police at the door. Of course, they didn't find me. After they'd left, Mom and I looked at each other with complicity, knowing that this "house call" was due to the people Dad had been working with for the past two years. I could never understand how he could associate with guys like those.

Mara came over. She brought me some winter clothes: it was cold up there. Ana and her husband came straight from City Hall. It dawned on me that I wasn't going to be able to go to Ana's wedding reception. After talking about it for so many months! I was even invited to the family dinner. I'd bought a new dress and some gorgeous shoes. They'd stay in my closet, never worn. Juan came over with a very affectionate little card, I really appreciated it.

The time came to leave for the airport. Mara and Laura took me. On the way we bought the paper. There was an article with the headline: "Heart Attack Kills Manuel Goldman on Plane En Route to Argentina." I burst into tears. It struck me as terrible that Dad should be a news item. He was my dad and nothing else. I remembered how I'd been to Ezeiza yesterday too, to meet Dad. Now I was back there, on my way to his funeral.

I don't know how I managed to board the plane. I didn't want to get to New York. I felt sure I would die on the plane too. That I wouldn't be able to stand it. That if Dad had died, I wanted to die too. I got a bit of sleep. I dreamed my cat was being strangled. A terrible injustice. I didn't know who could have even considered committing such an atrocity. I woke up terrified. I didn't want to sleep anymore.

In spite of me, we arrived. We landed. I had no choice but to get off the plane. I went through Immigration, got my suitcase, went through Customs. I was walking slowly. I knew the doors would open after a few more steps. I would see everyone. They were waiting for me to go to the funeral home. I didn't want those doors to open. Still, I kept walking. I saw them suddenly: Luis, Susana, her kids; I think her four kids were there. All dressed in black. I hugged Luis. We cried. I don't know if any words were spoken. There were tears, hugs. We went towards a taxi. It was really cold. I was coming from the summer, I was tanned. They were white, really white, pale. I looked out at the road from the airport to Manhattan. It was all covered in snow. I couldn't believe that this time I wasn't going to visit Dad but to go to his funeral. That I'd never visit him again. I'd made this trip with him so many times, happy to see each other again. No one said anything, maybe there was nothing to say. All that pain drove off any words, made us mute.

We went to Dad's house. I asked Luis if he'd spoken to Elena. Elena was Mom's sister who lived in Switzerland. No. He hadn't told her yet. She was very important to me. I know she'd also be chose to Dad. In Buenos Aires I wouldn't even mention her name to Mom. They'd fallen out seven years ago. They didn't speak to each other. I felt like a delinquent for loving my aunt.

They told me the wake wasn't going to be at Dad's house. The funeral home was far away. Everyone was going over there. I should wear black. I didn't have any black clothes. I had jeans and a sweater on. They told me that going dressed like that was disrespectful. I didn't understand why. There didn't seem to be any room for disagreement.

Luis had argued with Susana about whether the coffin should be open or closed. Susana preferred it to be open. Luis didn't. He didn't want to see Dad dead. I did. I wanted to see him for the last time. I wanted to say goodbye. Luis preferred to keep the memory of Dad when he was alive. I wanted both memories. After all, his death was part of him too. They decided the coffin would be closed but anyone who wanted to could open it.

Before going to the funeral home, Luis and I stopped at a store. I thought it was ridiculous for me to wear black; the last thing Dad ever paid any attention to was clothes. Anyhow, we went. I had a white T-shirt on. Luis was furious to see I wasn't wearing a bra. He ordered me categorically to buy one. I left the store dressed completely in black.

We arrived at a sumptuous building I'd never been to. It was in one of the most elegant neighborhoods of Manhattan. Everything seemed so remote. I felt like none of it had anything to do with me. Like that wasn't my place. Like that wasn't my dad.

There weren't very many people. It was a huge place. An entire floor with several large rooms. I saw Pablo, one of Susana's sons. He told us that Dad was already there. Someone had gone to Brazil to get the body. He died in that country where he didn't know anybody. Alone. They took him off the plane in São Paulo. They took him to a hospital. But by then there was nothing they could do. Pablo pointed out the room he was in. He asked us if we wanted to see him. I wanted to. Luis didn't. The room was very big. The coffin was at the far end. Pablo and I went up to it. He opened it and we saw Dad's corpse. It didn't look like Dad.

I

They had painted his face pink. His expression was relaxed and vacant, lost. I recognized him by the hands. They were Dad's hands. And by the hair. It was his hair too. Over the last couple of years, he'd gone gray. He looked calm. Dad didn't seem to have noticed his death.

Two hours went by. More people kept coming. Most of them, unknown to me. Some of them, according to Luis, very important. But I didn't know who they were. Everything was so strange: that place, those people, Dad's wretched death.

I didn't have any friends there or anyone I felt close to. Susana and her kids weren't my family. They were Dad's family. Suddenly I saw Mom's friend Gloria. What a relief! Finally, someone I knew.

That day I did nothing but cry and walk around that horrible place, with its stifling heating, as impersonal as a hotel. You couldn't even go out for a walk, it was too cold. But at one point I felt practically suffocated and decided to go out. I went for a drink with some friends of Dad's. I'd known them since I was little. They'd been his students in the Physics Department. They were the only people I felt comfortable with after Gloria left. I didn't want to eat anything. Luis ordered a hamburger. Even the thought of food turned my stomach.

I don't know how I ended up at the Metropolitan Museum. I had a very strange feeling on the way into the museum. I thought how no one knew me. No one knew I was mourning my dad. It seemed the most fitting place to be at that moment. No one spoke there. An immense respectful silence reigned.

I bought some postcards with reproductions of paintings I liked. I sent one to Laura and one to Ana. I felt as if it were a way of sharing this with them.

Back there, I looked out the window. I saw it was night-time. People were starting to leave. Finally, just Susana, her kids, Luis and I were left. We wanted to say our last good-byes to Dad. There came a time when I couldn't take any more and wanted to have it over with once and for all. See him for the last time. Maybe say something to him. Promise him something. It was my last chance to see him. Never again. I said goodbye to Dad without telling him anything other than what he'd always known: that I loved him a lot and that I'd always remember him, always.

We ate in a restaurant: Susana, her kids, Luis, a childhood friend of Dad's and I. Inés, Susana's daughter, cried and said she wasn't hungry. I was hungry, I hadn't eaten a thing for two days.

Luis told me how he'd been planning a business trip with Dad for a long time. It would have been their first trip together. He started to cry when he said it and couldn't finish telling me. By then we were at home and about to go to bed. Luis was embarrassed for crying. I knew he believed his duty was to control himself. Act like an older brother. Protect me. Not show weakness. But he couldn't. I cried too. I felt so sorry for him. I thought life had been really unfair. It had taken Dad away from us all of a sudden. With no warning. We hardly slept at all that night. I got up early. I walked all around the house. I sat in an armchair to look around at what had been Dad's house.

There was no respite from the pain. That morning Elena called us. We finally got to speak to her! She said she'd found out through one of our cousins who lived in Spain, who'd heard from a scientist. "Luz, I'm crying too."

Dad was going to be buried in a cemetery in a resort town, near the beach, two hours away from Manhattan.

Dad had a cottage there. Everyone thought the cemeteries in New York were gloomy. As if the ones at the beach were cheerful! But to me, deep down, it didn't really matter. We would bury him in a non-denominational cemetery. It was explained that people of any religion could be buried there. I realized that religion became very important when someone died. The dead had to be honored in some way. Religions, with their rites, took care of this. It seemed like dying was even sadder for atheists. One invoked God in the face of this terrible pain. I would have liked to believe in God at that moment. But I never had believed and couldn't ask him for anything. Dad had been an atheist, of Jewish origin, and Susana was Catholic. They decided that a Jewish friend of Dad's would say a few words in Hebrew. Something had to be done and it didn't make any sense to call a rabbi. Better to keep it among friends... A chauffeur came to pick us up in a very long black car. We all sat in the back. We stopped by the funeral home. Lots of cars were leaving from there, all black, a long, long procession. We advanced slowly along the road.

We arrived at the cemetery. It was big and open, peaceful. The tombstones, covered in snow, were almost invisible. Despite the immense sadness, the place seemed pretty to me. We waited till all the people arrived. Then, from the car that headed the procession, they took out the coffin. They put it down on the ground and it sank into the snow a little. The grave was nearby, they'd already dug it, everything was ready.

Luis, Susana's three sons—Pablo, Andrés and José— and two friends of Dad's carried the coffin to the grave. I watched closely. I felt like I was starring in a movie: the snowy cemetery, with people dressed in mourning around the tombstones. There were only two colors: the white of the snow and the black of the clothes. No one said a word, it was scary. Susana went up to her sons to tell them they should feel honored to be carrying Dad's coffin. It seemed really heavy. I thought they'd never be able to lift it.

They lowered the coffin slowly to the bottom of the grave. I couldn't believe there was a body in there. I couldn't believe my dad was in there. Someone I didn't know said a prayer in Hebrew and another in English. I heard it from very far away. At that moment, the sun came out. The snow sparkled for an instant. Then it clouded over again. They started to cover the coffin. I didn't want them to. I didn't want them to cover the coffin with earth. But that's how they do it. I threw a handful of earth too. I said goodbye again. That was the last time. Final. We all embraced and cried as if we hadn't been crying for days. Dad stayed buried in Southampton and I knew that a part of me stayed with him. That even if I didn't want it, even though I lived so far away from Southampton, this place was mine too.

We went to Dad's cottage. Dad really liked this place. Since it was winter, everything was desolate. The trees were completely bare. The cottage was very cold. Some water had frozen in the sink. I went to Dad's room. On his bedside table I found the book he'd been reading: *Out of My Later Years,* by Albert Einstein. I skimmed over the page where the bookmark was. Had Dad known he was going to die before finishing this book? I put it in my purse. I kept it without telling anyone. From Dad's room I called Laura in Buenos Aires. I told her I'd be back the next day.

While we were there, I found out that José, Susana's youngest son, had gone back out to the cemetery with some friends. That made me really mad. Why had he gone back when he didn't even like Dad. They'd never gotten along. For sure José had wished him dead more than once.

In the afternoon we went back to Manhattan. I was tired. I didn't have the strength left to cry. Or to do anything. I felt empty. I took off the black clothes. The funeral uniform. Bit by bit I became myself again. But I knew I'd never be the same. That I'd always carry the stamp of that first of March.

The next day I went back to Buenos Aires. Luis came with me. He told me he felt like spending a few days in Mom's house. That New York would be really hard without Dad. I took, along with the Einstein book, another that Dad had been reading in the apartment in New York. I didn't take the bookmarks out of either of them. In amongst Einstein's reflections, I put an article from *The New York Times* which related the death of Manuel

Goldman and had a picture of him. And one from *Clarín* entitled: "Great Argentinian Physicist Dies." Among other things, it said that, "In 1969, he was dismissed from his post as Director of the National Astronomical Observatory for taking part in a general strike."

Dad loved being mentioned in the papers. I suppose he'd never imagined his death would cause such a stir. I didn't want to take anything else. What else could I want? I wanted my dad. I couldn't care less about the rest.

Susana came with us to the airport. I took my leave of New York. It would never be the same for me. It had taken away my dad and kept him confined there. My heart was eternally divided. We boarded the plane in silence, exhausted from so much pain.

Just as Dad had done a few days before, we woke up on the airplane. He to die, we to go on living. We knew it would be difficult. That now we wouldn't have Dad.

We felt completely grief-stricken. We knew our only consolation was to have each other.

We talked about the hard times to come. We were frightened that no one would love us now that we were fatherless. Luis asked me if I thought a girl could like a guy who didn't have a dad. In spite of everything, life went on. We promised we'd never fight and we'd always help each other. Through the little window, just visible, appeared Buenos Aires.

II

We had to spend Tuesdays, Thursdays and weekends at Dad's place. Did I ever hate that new apartment he'd recently moved into! It was still under construction. I had the feeling they'd never finish building it. It was really cold.

Luis and I slept in the same room. A huge room. A few times I heard Dad say there'd be two rooms, but in the end they didn't build the dividing wall. Who knows why not. It made me really mad. I wanted to have my own room. The apartment walls were painted white. They were spotless, no pictures or anything. Even though Dad put furniture in, it never got any homely warmth. It lacked Mom's touch, it lacked Ester.

Every Tuesday and Thursday, Dad came to pick us up. Luis and I waited on the steps outside the door. We went to eat in a restaurant. Always the same one. I always ordered the same dish. In the summer, we had an extra activity. After dinner, we went for ice cream.

I took a little bag with clothes for the next day. At Dad's place, I had a pair of pyjamas and a few toys, but the closets of our room seemed empty. I was really scared of Dad. One day he seemed strange, and I asked, "Daddy, why are you sad?" "Well," he answered, "living alone sometimes makes me sad."

His apartment struck me as uninhabitable, no matter how hard Dad tried to make us feel okay there. It was like a stage he set up and then took down when we left. Our beds were the ones that go one underneath the other. I got the bottom one. But they were placed in opposite corners of the room. My bed had little wheels. The blankets were ugly and prickly, not like the ones on my own bed. That wasn't my bed.

I didn't take baths at Dad's place. Before leaving home, Ester helped me take a bath and wash my hair. Dad thought a girl of six, almost seven, ought to be able to wash her own hair.

The next morning, Dad would wake us up early to go to school. It was so cold I didn't want to get out of bed. There was an electric heater. It made no difference at all. I shivered until we left. We went down to the garage, where it was much colder. We got into the car quickly. Luis and I fought over who got to sit up front beside Daddy.

Saturday nights were different. Since we didn't have to get up early the next morning, Dad told me stories in bed. Just me. Usually they were continuous. My favorite was the astronaut series. It was about a trip to the moon. When they landed, as had already been proven, they didn't see anything spectacular. The moon turned out to be a complete disappointment. A dry desert-like place. There were no extra-terrestrials, no uncommon stones, nothing of any interest. Even so, one of the astronauts decided to go down for a look. They got out a big ladder and down he climbed to the lunar surface. The rocket must have been enormous, so tall, I thought, while Dad gesticulated more and more enthusiastically. No sooner had he stepped onto the moon than he disappeared, right before the eyes of the other astronauts. No one understood what had happened. The rest of the crew were starting to panic. They speculated over what could have happened. They found themselves face to face with a seemingly unsolvable mystery. Finally they decided that another of the astronauts should go down a few rungs to see if he could find any clues to what had happened. When he did, he realized that the other astronaut hadn't disappeared but had become minuscule. It wasn't true that there were no inhabitants on the moon. There were tiny—almost microscopic—beings. They reached the conclusion that the surface of the moon had the virtue of shrinking earthlings. Just by touching it, they became minute.

After listening to the episodes of the long story about the astronauts, my nights became more difficult. I couldn't bring myself to get out of bed to go to the bathroom. Sometimes I'd wake up in the middle of the night dying for a pee. I'd turn on the night light and look at the floor. It was white. The kind they put in kids' rooms, made of some kind of easy to clean vinyl material. I was scared to get out of bed. I was convinced I would become minuscule. And so, feeling like I'd die from needing to pee so bad, I wouldn't get up. I'd lean over the side of the bed and look at the floor for a long time. I'd put out my hand, but couldn't bring myself to touch it.

In the morning I'd wake up huddled in a corner of the bed. I was still afraid to get down. That white floor seemed dangerous. It was like ice. I waited until Dad came in the room. After he walked on the white floor and didn't become teeny-tiny, I'd get up. But sometimes Dad didn't come to wake me up. I called him. I asked him to please come. I didn't tell him I was scared to get up, that was embarrassing. I shouted and shouted until Dad came. When I saw him come into the room, walk across the floor, and not become small, then I could get out of bed.

III

My grandparents (Mom's parents) had bought a new apartment in Punta del Este. Mom decided we'd go for a few days. I was twelve. Going into seventh grade. Mom and my grandma Clara did nothing but fight. It was not a very good idea for us to be together. Although I never lost the hope that maybe some day we'd get along.

On the other hand, Mommy got along really well with her sister, Elena. They were really close. I loved Elena a lot too. She was a few years younger than Mom. They both taught English, were super thin and had the same tone of voice. Some of the time they worked together: they gave classes at the same firm. Elena came over to our house for lunch on days they went there. I wanted those lunches to go on forever. Elena was single then, so Ester called her Niña Elena. During those lunches, I was happy.

Elena was a *peronista*. She was with the *Montoneros*. She was a grass-roots activist. She always talked to Mommy about her political activities. I didn't understand a thing.

But I loved listening to everything they said. They talked about a *peña*. Elena lived on Peña street, so I thought it was something that was happening in her building. I realized it wasn't. It was about some meetings. Elena told how at those meetings, their real names were kept secret. They used nicknames. The one I liked best was Cacho Ropero—Big Joe Wardrobe. Elena talked about the university too. Running away from the cops, chanting slogans, the General. The General was always in the conversations. And the Uncle. Later they talked about arms. It seemed like people went to these peñas armed. Elena always criticized Mom for sending us to a private school. She and Mom had gone to St. Catherine's. I didn't see anything wrong with English schools. Elena said that when she had children, she'd send them to a public school and to karate lessons, because it was an excellent form of self-defence.

I was a *peronista* too. I was. I was nine years old and a *peronista*. To me the *Montos* were a group of friends. I was fond of them. Mom and Ester were *peronistas*. But much less fervently. They weren't activists. Ester had met Evita. Evita had been to her village in Santiago del Estero. Ester had never forgotten her. Dad was the complete opposite: anti-*peronista*. He said the whole thing was a big lie. He didn't believe them. He hadn't voted for Perón.

My grandfather was a lawyer. Terribly serious. At every election he voted for the most conservative candidate. But I really loved him. My grandparents' house was the opposite of mine. It was different from Dad's too. I hardly ever slept at my grandparents' house. The times I did I was completely surprised because my grandfather would take me to school and before I got out of the car, he'd ask me if I had some cash. I never knew what I had. I'd look. Sometimes I'd say yes, I had just enough for the bus. My grandfather told me that wasn't sufficient. I should have some more. "Just in case." I'd never heard that from my parents. What did "just in case" mean? In case of what? It scared me that "just in case." I didn't know what cases he was talking about. Maybe my parents didn't know about them.

I didn't want to go to Punta del Este that summer. I wanted to go to Villa Gesell. But I didn't tell Mom.

My grandmother was alone in Punta del Este. My grandfather stayed in Buenos Aires working at his law firm. The first day, things went pretty well. Clara and Mom seemed to be putting up with each other. Being in my grandmother's house was like enlisting in the army. There were schedules for everything. For getting up, for breakfast. It didn't matter that we were supposed to be on vacation. No skipping meals. You couldn't eat at the beach because you'd spoil your appetite for lunch. I was dying for a hotdog but Clara wouldn't let me. It was obvious that at this rate we wouldn't last two days without punching each other out. Luis and I weren't used to that regimen. On the third day the quarrels exploded. Mommy and Clara didn't stop shouting. Mom did everything in the way Clara found most annoying. She broke down her order. Clara got really edgy. Mom was never hungry at the time my grandmother decided we had to be. Luis couldn't stand Clara's orders either but they argued less. But after a very short time, we couldn't put up with it anymore.

Clara said that everything was really expensive. That you couldn't even set foot inside a restaurant. One day we went downtown. Clara wanted to see a hotel that had been renovated. The Palace. According to Clara, anyone who stayed there had to be a millionaire.

The situation in the house deteriorated. Mommy left. Luis and I stayed with Clara. I was bored. I didn't have a single friend. I was having a terrible time. I didn't understand why they'd decided to go to Punta del Este. Clara told me to knit a sweater. She would teach me. I felt like the most unfortunate person on the planet. The middle of summer in Punta del Este and me knitting on the balcony. Each afternoon I spent watching the house across the street. It seemed much nicer than mine. The kids were blond there. I couldn't see when we'd ever get to go back to Buenos Aires. To meet up with my friends again.

One day, while we were having dinner, there was a phone call from Buenos Aires: my grandfather had been rushed into surgery. Clara burst into tears on the telephone. Luis hugged her. I didn't. Clara was really worried. Pedro was very apprehensive. She told us she was going to Buenos Aires immediately. And what about us? We'd have to call Dad and Susana. They were in La Paloma, on vacation together for the first time. We had to ask them to come and pick us up.

Susana arrived in a rage. For once they got to spend their vacation alone together and we come along and spoil her plans. The last thing I wanted to do was to ruin their vacation. It wasn't my fault things had happened the way they did.

I felt unwanted. I always felt unwanted. Out of place. A pain in the neck. Susana regarded us with hatred. Dad tried to overlook it. I tried not to be a bother. After a few days, Daddy and Susana decided that Inés should come too. Inés was sixteen. She'd been going out with Leo for a month. We were staying at the Palace. The one we'd visited with my grandmother and was supposedly for millionaires. I'd never realized I was a millionaire. But at the time, the last thing on my mind was the hotel. Leo had a huge house in Punta del Este. Inés said it was great that we were staying at the Palace. Daddy and Susana were together. Inés, with her boyfriend, Luis, with his friends, and me, with my sweater. But the teacher had changed: Susana had now replaced my grandmother.

Pablo, Andrés and José were spending the vacation with their dad. Susana talked about them constantly. Leo hadn't even met them. Susana declared, "You'll see, once you get to know them..." Inés went on about how exotic Leo was: "He lives in a mansion in San Isidro and has a Swiss bank account." Since manners meant nothing to him, Leo went to eat in the most expensive restaurants in Buenos Aires with no shoes on. I didn't see what was so fascinating about walking down the street barefoot. But if they said so, it must be. I thought I was an idiot: I didn't understand anything and had nothing to tell.

Each day we went to a different beach. Always far away from the hotel. It didn't seem like the same place I'd been vacationing with my mom and grandmother. Daddy and Susana saw everything differently. Places that Mom liked, Dad didn't, and vice versa. After a little while, I'd have two different versions of the same place. I didn't like either one. Both made me feel bad. Dad's, much worse.

We went back on the ferry. I finished the sweater on board. Susana tried it on right away. Later I tried it. It was too big for me. But it looked good on her.

Once we got to Buenos Aires, Dad took us home. We met Mom downstairs. She was going out in a big rush. Furious. She barely said hello. She told us that Pedro had died. I was stunned. Grandpa Pedro, dead? How could that be?

It wasn't the first time a close relative had died. Dad's older brother had passed away three years earlier. But Daddy didn't want us, the kids, to go to the funeral. Mom didn't agree with Dad. For her, there was nothing to hide. So, when Grandpa Pedro died, I had to go to the cemetery.

Instead of making me sad, Pedro's death angered me. Clara was really upset. She said there were tons of paperwork to do and ran around like a madwoman. I didn't understand what was going on. I wanted to do something for my grandfather. I thought of buying him a beautiful bouquet of flowers from around the corner. But I didn't. Too many people had brought flowers. So I decided that, to pay tribute to my grandfather, I'd wear my hair the way he liked it, in a ponytail. It seemed like the best thing I could do for him. My grandfather was a man of few words. But every time he saw me he told me I was prettier and that I should wear my hair tied back.

They held the wake for my grandfather in the dining room of his apartment. In one corner was a friend of Pedro's sitting on his own. He looked truly sad. I didn't cry at all. The next day, we went to the Tablada cemetery. It was a Jewish funeral. I got mad. One time Pedro said that when he died, not to give him a religious funeral. I got mad at my grandmother. She couldn't even respect her husband's death.

I didn't see Mommy cry once. I heard her say she was so sad she didn't want to wear any colorful clothes. It seemed to me that Pedro had been very old and that Mommy was too big to get sad. A very good friend of Mom's came back from her weekend house to visit as soon as she heard Pedro had died. I didn't understand why someone should come running because Grandpa died either.

A few days after Pedro's death, Mom started arguing with Elena and Clara. I felt lonelier all the time. Lost and lonely. On top of everything, Ester wasn't there. Ester had gone to

Santiago del Estero to spend the holidays with her mom like she did every year in December. But it was already February and she wasn't back. She never took more than three weeks. I missed her so much. Why didn't she come back? She didn't even send me a card. A relative of hers was filling in for her at home. I didn't like her. I wanted Ester to come back. Soon. One afternoon I heard the back doorbell. I looked out and saw Ester. I ran out to hug her. I burst into tears. I squeezed her so tight, my arms barely reaching around her. I didn't want her to go away ever again. She explained she'd just come back for a visit, that she still wasn't coming back home. I begged her to please come back soon. She answered me asking what I wanted her for when there was already a girl in the house. I felt even worse. Seeing me so shocked, Ester smiled and said it was only a joke.

For my ninth birthday, Dad gave me a Siamese kitten. I adored him. I was taking piano lessons so I wrote a song for him. I played it all the time. At Dad's they had a Siamese, too. It belonged to Inés. We both played with him. He was always sniffing me: he smelled my cat. One Sunday night, coming home and seeing Mom's face, I knew something bad had happened. I asked after my cat, Chacho. Mommy looked at me gravely. Chacho had died. I cried inconsolably. Mom told me he'd taken sick, she called the vet's but there was nothing they could do. Chacho had eaten roach poison. I couldn't stop crying. I went to the laundry room. There he was, dead, in his box. Mom tried to console me but I could not be consoled. Mommy loved Chacho, too. She said that Siamese cats were very frail. Elena came over, She was as sad as we were over Chacho. Elena had given me a book about cats. We decided to bury Chacho. Elena had a car, and the Panamerican highway struck us as a good place. We went in the Fiat 600. Mom, Elena, Luis and I and the box with the dead cat. This was at the time of the guerrillas so Elena warned us that we'd have to be careful. It could look suspicious for four people to get out of a car at the side of the Panamerican with shovels and a box. We buried him in front of the Nestle's factory.

The next day Ester came to wake me up. I had to go to school. I was still crying. Ester hugged me. She said I shouldn't cry so much, that I could get another one. That those cats were too delicate. But I didn't want another, I wanted Chacho. I felt like crying at school too. I would never sing the song I wrote for Chacho again. His death grieved me and I would never get over it. I hated the dead. When any relative died, I hated them. At those times my parents forgot about me. When my Grandpa Pedro died, Mom died for everything and everyone. Except for fighting with her mom and her sister over the inheritance.

A few weeks after Pedro died, I arranged to have lunch with Clara one afternoon. Laura's father came to pick her up from school so he gave me a lift too. I got out of the car a couple of blocks from my grandmother's place. One of the blocks was a long one. I saw all kinds of police. It had been a month since Isabel Perón had been ousted. The atmosphere seemed strange. They'd put up a barricade at the corner. I walked along really scared. Not rushing. I didn't want them to see me. From a distance, a policeman was motioning to me. It looked like he was telling me to get out of there, or to run. I kept on as if I hadn't seen. I was getting more and more frightened. I didn't want to go back. I hadn't done anything. I arrived at my grandmother's place absolutely terrified. Clara wasn't home. The maid let me in. She said Clara would be there any minute. The phone rang. I answered: it was Mom. She told me to leave Grandma's place right that minute and come home. I thought Mom knew what was going on outside with the police. I asked her if something bad had happened. Mom got all upset. "I don't want you to eat there!" she shouted. "Come home!" I asked her again if something was going on but she didn't answer me. "I don't want you eating there!" she insisted. Without explaining anything to the maid, I left.

Mommy always arrived home fuming about her quarrels with Clara. Even if I told her I'd done the worst thing in the world, she'd keep on about her obsession, nothing else mattered. I even knew that to get out of talking about myself with my mom, all I had to do was ask her something about Clara. As time went on I felt I mattered less and less. Mom had started legal proceedings against my grandmother over the estate.

Dad had lots of hassles too. In March, 1976 the military had taken power. Dad was considered left-wing. He received constant threats. The year before, the Triple A, the most notorious of the right-wing death squads, had come looking for him, but he wasn't home. I knew almost nothing of my parents' ideological and political lives. All I knew is they paid less and less attention to me.

Elena and Guille had had Esteban the year before. When he was about to be born, Mom, Luis and I went to the hospital. We had to wait for ages. They hadn't even taken Elena into the delivery room. Since my uncle Guille was a neonatologist, he stayed with her the whole time. I peeked into the room. I saw an enormous belly covered by a white sheet and Guille motioned for me to get out. I realized they were going to be a while. Tired of waiting, we went home before the baby was even born. Later they told us it was a boy and they'd called him Esteban.

The birth had been by caesarian section, and my aunt, who wasn't altogether well, asked me if I could take her dog for a walk each day. It was December. I didn't have to go to school. I was happy to do as Elena asked. Every morning I went to their house, stayed there for a little while and then took the dog to the park. "Take her out for at least an hour," Elena requested. I took Tintín books and let the dog play where she liked. I was thrilled to be Elena and Guille's niece. I felt proud of my little cousin. He was very fair and had gray eyes. Elena said it was lucky he was born in December so she didn't have to keep him all bundled up. I, in the meantime, learned things about babies. I'd never seen a mother breast-feeding her baby. And I felt important. I had a real cousin and they needed me to look after the dog.

Three months after Esteban's birth, Grandpa Pedro died. Soon after, I stopped seeing Elena, Guille and Esteban. The following summer Luis went to Switzerland. My aunt and uncle were living there. They had left in a hurry. After the *coup d'état* in '76, my aunt was frightened because of her *peronista* activism. Even though she hadn't been a guerrilla, she knew that the soldiers weren't making any distinctions when they took people. Luis told me that Elena knew I'd started my period. I couldn't for the life of me imagine how she could have found that out, we didn't even get to say good-bye when they left to live in Europe.

IV

I started to get tits when I was ten. They worried me a lot. I didn't want to be big, not for anything in the world. I wanted to stop growing. I was horrified. I tried on clothes endlessly until finding what best hid my tits or I flattened them with my bikini top. I was extremely jealous of girls who hadn't started to develop yet.

My school friends and I started talking about sexual matters in fifth grade. I was convinced that for a woman to get pregnant, she had to have sex while she had her period. The girls in my grade asked me how a woman knew she was going to get her period. That, I didn't know. Since the subject was being discussed so much, the teachers decided to give us a lesson on sex education. The idea was to clear up any doubts. It didn't clear up a single one for me: no one understood the words they used or the slides they showed. I didn't want to become a woman. Let other girls become women. Susana's sons and Luis teased Inés because she had a boyfriend and big tits. They didn't even look at me. I was one of the boys. Of the six of us, Inés was the only woman. There wasn't room for another. She was slender and pretty. I was ugly. No boy would notice me.

Dad's house was like another school. When we were bad, Dad punished us the same way as the principal did. He'd make us be quiet. And to make matters worse, all of us at the same time. Not even then did he pay attention to just me. Dad said that Inés was the only one who helped around the house. She was his favorite. The rest of us were a bunch of slackers. Not even capable of setting the table. I hated being part of the mob. I hated Inés. I envied absolutely everything about her. She was the only woman I envied.

Susana amused herself giving us sex education lessons. She went on and on explaining what menopause was. I knew it by heart. She told us to ask her any questions at all. And I felt like I was back at school.

My friends and I discussed our mothers' ages when they'd started menstruating. Mara said hers started when she was nine. I said my mom was fifteen. But it wasn't true. In reality, I hadn't asked her. I almost never talked about sex with Mom. Once I told her that for the mother of one of my friends making love was a basic necessity. It wasn't like that for Mom. I told her they'd explained it as being similar to the need for food. Mom got mad. She shouted that it was a lie. That the two weren't comparable. That if I didn't believe her I should think about nuns and people who were separated. I believed Mom. She was separated and she slept in a bed like mine. Dad and Susana never said anything about whether it was a necessity or a pleasure, as I'd heard somewhere else. They talked about it as something to do to have babies and nothing more. I thought, on the one hand, that Dad and Susana, since they didn't have any children, must not have sex. But, on the other hand, I'd also heard that married people, even without kids, did it.

The boys in my class gossiped about girls stuffing their bras with cotton batting. It struck me as ridiculous. I explained that we didn't want to have tits. That they were completely mistaken. But there was no convincing them.

I didn't want to start getting my period. Just as I imagined Mom not starting hers until she was fifteen, I believed the same would happen to me. But in any case, I realized that Mom and I were different. We had very different bodies, Mom was a rake, I was more shapely. But I was embarrassed at being better built than Mom. Although, at the same time, I liked it. I never wanted it to be apparent that I was her daughter. When I was little and Ester used to take me to the square, people would ask her if I was hers. She said no. "Go on, say you're my mom," I begged. Mom never took me to the square. I would rather have been

Ester's daughter. At school, they thought Ester was my mom, too. She walked me there and came to pick me up. Mom was blond with green eyes. I, on the other hand, had dark hair and eyes. People could never believe I was her child. Luis was blond. He was definitely Mom's. I was the ugly one in the family. The black sheep. People asked me why I wasn't blond, or why didn't I have green eyes like Mom, or wasn't skinny like Inés, or didn't live with Dad, like Susana.

On the weekends, at Dad's place in the country, I always played with the boys. At night, we played hide-and-seek. This was my chance to hide with one of Andrés' friends, who I liked. But he didn't pay any attention to me, he didn't realize I hid with him on purpose. One Saturday, we watched a movie on television. It was about a couple. The man, much older than his wife. Dad advised me never to get involved with men much older than me. It would cause me trouble. The only nice thing about weekends in the country was staying up late staring at the flames in the fireplace. I could spend hours watching the fire and daydreaming. It seemed to enclose something marvellous. It hypnotized me. Dad sold that place two years after buying it. He bought a weekend place with more land in Lujan. We were bigger by then. Relations had worsened. Inés would only go if her boyfriend came. Luis, with his friends. Andrés and José had made friends with the neighbors, who were all boys. I didn't know what to do. My only choice was to play with them. Be a boy, again. The guys told me that the workers who were putting in the pool said that I was prettier than Inés. I didn't believe them, I was sure it was a joke.

The first summer we had the place, Susana's kids spent January there. I went on the weekends. One Saturday, I arrived with my hair cut short and a new pair of pants. I'd gone to the hairdresser's with Mom. Dad and Susana didn't like my hair cut and they thought my pants were too dressy for the country.

After sixth grade, my body changed. I suddenly discovered I had a perfect waist and a woman's ass. It was embarrassing to wear pants. I didn't want to be seen from behind. I had one pair that were really tight. Mom thought they fit perfectly.

One time, when we were at the weekend place of a friend of Mom's, I discovered I'd grown little hairs in my armpits. I thought they were horrid. What anguish! It was terrifying. Irremediable. I didn't tell anyone. I thought they'd laugh at me.

I found a book on sex education in Dad's house. There was a picture of a naked adolescent. You could see his willy and it had hairs around it. That photo startled me and I shut the book quickly. But later I wanted to look at it again. I searched the shelves for that book several times. I couldn't find it. I was dying to see that picture again.

It was normal for Susana's kids to walk around the house in their underwear. Especially Pablo. He went to the shower with a little towel around his waist; it was always falling off. I took advantage to take a peek. I never managed to see much. But I loved it. It was great to see Pablo in his little towel.

During seventh grade I suffered like crazy under the threat of starting my period. I prayed to God not to get it. I was terrified. Once I found a stain in my panties. But it wasn't blood. I asked Susana what discharge was. She wanted to know if I'd had some. I said no. That I was just wondering.

When we were twelve, Mara and I were really into clothes. We tried on her mother's dresses. Mara wore high heels. She explained that they made you look thinner. We started liking boys from other schools. We met them at parties. One time we went into Mara's parents' bathroom; she showed me a little case shaped like an oyster: inside was a round rubber thing. "This is the condom my folks use for fucking." I was a bit taken aback by the shape of it. Mara told me that they put it in between the two of them. I didn't understand at all. Nor did I ask.

I felt more comfortable at Mara's place than anywhere else. One day she told me she'd grown little hairs in her armpits and her mom had given her a cream to get rid of them. Mara said that when we got older, we'd have to do it with wax. She asked if I had underarm hair too. I said yes. I couldn't believe I could get rid of those hairs. I cut the pussy ones off with scissors but I didn't tell anyone. Once I got rid of the ones in my armpits, I could say I hadn't got any yet.

Moni never lent me her clothes. She didn't tell me anything about what it was like to be a woman either. I didn't ask her. I hated her and didn't want to be like her.

The dreaded day came when I got my first period. I kept it secret. But Mom noticed. She came into my room when I was already in bed. She asked me if I had something to tell her. I answered no, although I knew exactly what she was getting at. She insisted. I told her no again. She told me she knew I'd started menstruating. I covered my mouth with the sheet and said, "Oh yeah." She asked me to take the sheet off my mouth so she could hear me. I didn't want her to hear me. I didn't move the sheet. I just wanted her to get out of my room as soon as possible. She asked me why I hadn't told her. I didn't want to answer her.

One day in the country, it was really hot. The pool was full and I had my period. I was the only one who didn't want to put on a bathing suit. Everyone asked me why. I answered that I didn't feel like swimming in the pool. No way I was going to tell them the truth. I'd die of embarrassment. In the evening they were all tanned. I was the only pale one. I felt uglier than ever.

During seventh grade, Mara and I spent all day every day together. Boys were our constant topic of conversation. We both wanted to have a boyfriend. Mara's parents, and her younger sisters, went to their place in the country every weekend. Sometimes they let Mara stay in Buenos Aires. I'd ask Dad to let me stay with Mom. Then Mara and I could go to parties together on Saturday nights.

One weekend, Mom didn't want me staying with her. But there was a party, and I wasn't going to miss it. It didn't bother me that Mom objected to me staying home. The problem was easy to solve. I told Dad I was staying with Mom; her that I was going out to the country. Mara told her parents she was coming to my Dad's weekend house with me and on Saturday night, after the party, we'd go sleep at Dad's. I had a spare key to his place. We were sure that during the weekend, there wouldn't be anyone home at Dad's. We thought it was a perfect plan.

The party was in a neighborhood we didn't know. At about three in the morning we decided to leave. It was our first time on our own in such a faraway place. We walked a few blocks. We looked at the numbers of the buses at the stops but didn't find a single one we recognized. Dad's house was in Belgrano. We had no idea how to get there. But we weren't scared. We thought it was fun. Two guys showed up who'd been at the party and also lived in Belgrano. We decided to share a taxi. We had a feeling it would cost us a fortune. When we got out at Dad's, Mara and I were left without a cent. The guys kept going.

I tried to open the door and couldn't. We tried several times with no luck. We started to get worried. It was four in the morning and we didn't have a cent. I noticed the door was locked and bolted, and we didn't have a key for that lock. We considered walking to Mom's but we didn't know the way. We'd never made that journey on foot. Another possibility was to sleep in the doorway and ask people in the street for change the next day. We scrapped that idea: it was too cold. In the meantime, we kept putting in and taking out the key. Unexpectedly, someone asked, "Who is it?" I thought maybe it was Inés. "It's Mara and Luz." Carla, Pablo's girlfriend, opened the door. I felt my heart start beating again. Carla told us we were crazy. Pablo had lied too. They thought he was at Carla's family's weekend place. The four of us sat up talking in Pablo's room for a while. They asked us what we were doing there at that hour. Carla was treating us as if we were little girls when she was only a few months older than us. She was in her first year at high school. At dawn, Mara and I went to sleep in my room.

Mom and Dad found out about the lie. I didn't know how. Much less, how they both managed to find out when they didn't even speak to each other. But they didn't tell me off.

In September of that year I got together with Mario. Right away Pablo commented pointedly: "Carla knows your boyfriend." The day after he told me he liked me, I went sailing with Mom and her partner. She'd been going out with him for five years. I went to pieces in the boat. I didn't eat anything all day. I was so worried. I couldn't stop thinking of the moment when Mario would kiss me. I'd kissed boys in my class before but never the real thing.

Mario got out of school earlier, so he came by to meet me. Mara was always getting in the way. I couldn't stand it. I asked her to please go away, to leave us in peace.

Pablo had a girlfriend, Inés had a boyfriend, Andrés had a girlfriend. It was vital for me to have a boyfriend too. Having a boyfriend who was in high school was my dream and Mario was only in grade seven. I thought high school guys were the greatest. Mara told me she was going to be introduced to a fifteen-year-old. I wanted the same. Mara said to me, "You've already got a boyfriend." But one day Mario went to camp, and a little while later I heard through the grapevine that he'd been with another girl there. I didn't want to see him anymore. He invited me to his birthday party in November anyway. It was a few days before mine. We were turning thirteen. I went but I didn't pay any attention to him. He and his brother lived with their mother. That's where they celebrated his birthday. I was curious to meet his mother. Mario told me his mom had made two suicide attempts: once she threw herself from the second story and the other, from the seventh. Mario told me at the house of one of his friends. We were on our own with the light off. I felt it was very painful for him to tell me.

As December approached, I felt lonelier and lonelier. It was sad to be finishing elementary school. Before the end of classes, I turned thirteen. I didn't want to celebrate. A few friends came over to visit. But I was sad. That day, as usual, I had lunch with Dad. I normally took that afternoon off school.

That time I didn't want to. Everyone thought it was strange that I was in school on my birthday. Mario came looking for me after the bell. But I wasn't interested in him anymore.

I daydreamed that on the last day of school I was going to cry a lot. I imagined it was the end of the world. We had two parties: one in school and another on the sports field. But I couldn't feel any sadness. I didn't spill a single tear. The last day of classes everyone was celebrating the end of the year outside. I hadn't decided whether to go out and was alone in the house. Ester said there were kids all over the place. I called Mara. She wasn't there. She'd already gone out to celebrate. I felt like an idiot sitting in the kitchen while everyone was having fun outside. I didn't want to celebrate the end of elementary school but I didn't want to be alone either.

For the holidays, Dad, Susana, her kids and I went to New York. We were there for over a month. Luis went to Punta del Este with Mom. Dad wanted to go and live in New York. He'd been offered a very good job.

One morning I got my period again. I decided it was time Dad and Susana knew. I'd rather tell Susana than Mom. Even more, I actually wanted to tell Susana. I thought she'd be nice to me. Early in the morning, I went to Dad and Susana's room. I was scared to knock on the door. When I was little I'd spend hours wandering around the house without getting up the nerve to knock. But this time I knocked and they told me to come in. They were already awake, which I thought strange. I felt something odd in the atmosphere but paid no attention. I told Susana I'd gotten my period for the first time. It was a lie but I'd been too embarrassed to tell them then. I was so used to lying that I did it naturally. Susana congratulated me. She was pleased. I pretended it made me happy too.

That night Dad came to our room. He told us my cousin Marcos had disappeared. I realized that was the reason they'd seemed strange that morning. I didn't know what he meant by *disappeared*. Dad said some policemen in civilian clothes had come looking for him. They claimed they wanted to ask him some questions before he started his military service. They promised my aunt that the next day he'd be where he was supposed to enlist. Nobody knew anything more about Marcos. Dad's face when he told us, "Marcos has disappeared," really made an impression on me. It was a mixture of rage and fatalism. Marcos was his only nephew. Inés said something about "habeas corpus." I didn't understand what that was. I didn't ask.

That trip was the first time we weren't obliged to go to museums. I couldn't believe it. But anyway, when I didn't go I felt horrible. Inés always went out with Susana. I, on the other hand, went for walks on my own. I bought clothes and didn't show them to anybody. I hid them so they wouldn't call me materialistic. I said I'd never wear a bra. I didn't even want to discuss it. On the other hand, I knew no one would buy me one. In one of the dozens of stores I was always hanging around, I went up to a rack with tons of bras hanging on it. I chose one. On the box was a picture of a girl my age. I bought it without trying it on. And that package, I hid more than anything else.

V

By the time I got to seventh grade, I was pretty sick of school. I wanted to leave. My two best friends and I decided to change schools, to go to a public one. Several kids in my class had switched that year. I thought it'd be good. Screw the board of the Instituto Horizonte. Let it go bust!

Mara, Laura and I landed in a school where everything was alien to us. We didn't even last two months.

I told Mom I wanted to go back to the Instituto Horizonte. She wouldn't let me. I freaked out. I screamed so much she finally gave in. Mara screamed too and her parents gave in as well. Laura's didn't. Mara and I went back. Laura stayed by herself at the public school. I felt really bad for her. Laura would have to spend every afternoon at home alone.

Our school had a double curriculum. In the mornings we were taught in Spanish. In the afternoons, we had English and other activities: music, chess and stuff like that. It all seemed like a farce to me. Mom always criticized the way they taught us English.

In the fifth grade reader, there was a questionnaire for writing a report on our parents. It had questions about things like where they'd met, where they'd gotten married, how they got along. I was alarmed when I saw it. When it came time to pose the questions I was even more alarmed. While Mom was drying her hair, I asked the questions. The hair dryer made a lot of noise. She answered in short sentences. I couldn't hear very well and neither could she. Finally, she told me that she and Dad had met in the United States. They got married in Chicago. My mom thought it was bad for them to have given us that reader. It was not very likely that all the parents would want to answer those questions.

I was embarrassed that Mom and Dad were separated. I said it didn't bother me, though, that it was all the same to me. That I wasn't going to whine about that. In my class there was another student whose parents had split up. She whined. She was sad. I hated her. I thought she was silly. My dad had married Susana by then. I felt lots of worse things had happened to me than my parents' separation. I'd always seen it as an indisputable fact. They'd split up when I was two. I didn't remember them together. More than that, it was difficult for me to imagine them ever having been married. I hated that girl who cried because her parents had split up.

She felt so sorry for her little brother. He was so little and already his parents had split up. I found this outrageous. I was sure no one had thought about how little I was when my parents split up. I preferred my parents being separated. It was a very advantageous situation. I could always do what I liked. Although I felt marginalized, I got a certain pleasure from this marginality. The mere act of imagining my parents together made me gasp. It was better the way it was. They were both mine but apart. Mom and Dad weren't just divorced, they never spoke to one another. They hated each other. They never got together. Not even to talk about us.

The certainty that my parents' separation hadn't affected me filled me with pride.

There were kids who started to do badly at school because of it. I was an excellent student. One of the best in my class. And I never cried.

Mom bought me *The Boys and Girls Book of Divorce*. I didn't want to read it. I saw it at Dad's house too. Susana had bought it for her kids. I saw a boy at school with it as well. I felt a certain complicity with him. And rejection at the same time. It didn't seem right to me that he should have it in among his schoolbooks. For me, having separated parents was an advantage over the other kids. They couldn't choose whether they wanted to be with their mom or with their dad. I could. I chose daily.

I worried about Mom and Dad seeing each other. It didn't happen often. Not even through school. Mom never set foot inside the school, not even for parent-teacher meetings or ceremonies. On days after meetings with the parents, my classmates would talk to the teacher about what had been said at home on the previous evening. I didn't have anything to say. Mine had never gone.

It was awful having to explain that my parents were separated. And that my dad was remarried, to a woman with four children from a previous marriage. "No, they're not my brothers and she's not my sister, no, I don't live with my dad, they live with my dad but they're not his kids, they're not related to me at all." Ever since I was in nursery school I'd been talking about parental separations. If someone said their parents weren't together, I'd ask them to be more specific: I wanted to know if they were separated or divorced. At that point, my parents were separated, but not legally. When Daddy was about to marry Susana, he wanted to get the division of property settled quickly. It was the first time in my life I heard talk of court cases and lawyers. Mom and Dad's settlement seemed very complicated. Dad wanted Luis and me to live with him. Mom wanted us with her. They reached an arrangement: we would spend alternate days in each house. Great solution! The documents obliged us to live divided lives.

In fifth grade, Laura was my best friend. We lived a block away from each other and both went home for lunch so we took the bus together. On the way we sang *Sui Géneris* songs. There was a line that went: "...in Recoleta." We liked it. That was our neighborhood.

We started to realize there were different parts to Buenos Aires. We knew the 110, that we took to school, ended up in Villa del Parque. But we got off at Canning and Paraguay. Past that, it was all a mystery. I loved it that Laura and I were neighbors. The *Sui Géneris* song went on: "... in keeping with its noble lineage." We wondered what lineage meant. Laura phoned me every lunchtime to make sure we were meeting at the bus stop at one. I felt happy singing with Laura on the bus.

Although Mom and Dad weren't together, Dad lived nearby. He'd moved several times but always within the same neighborhood. His first apartment with Susana and her kids was the one at Libertad and Alvear. It was a split-level flat. I hated it. The heating was stifling. In the mornings I woke up with a dry throat. I couldn't swallow. The only thing that helped was warm milk with Nesquik. I was horrified by the possibility there might not be any milk or any Nesquik. In Dad's apartment there were never any of the things I wanted. I was shocked if there wasn't milk for breakfast. I hated that apartment of Dad's more than all the rest. That didn't happen at mine. Ester always made sure there was enough of everything. In the mornings, she brought Nesquik to me in my room. Only Ester knew how to make it properly: not too hot, not too cold. Just the right temperature. And it wouldn't get a skin on top. Ester was perfect. Mom was not! Mom always made it too cold or she didn't put enough Nesquik in. She always did something wrong. I couldn't stand her. I wanted to kill her. It was incredible how she could never do anything right. How she never paid any attention to things she did for me.

Dad and Susana decided to move. They wanted a bigger place. The apartment on Libertad was brand new when they bought it. However, in no time at all, it was wrecked. The under-floor heating was so intense, the wooden floorboards had come up. I thought it was disgusting.

One Sunday they told me they were taking me to see a very nice house in Belgrano they were on the verge of buying. Dad thought Belgrano was a little far away. But, on the other hand, he liked the idea of living in a house with a garden. I was delighted at the prospect. I loved the house on Virrey Loreto Street in Belgrano. I got excited about the move. However, my enthusiasm did not last long. The realization of Dad's plans never failed to disappoint me. They seemed great, and then, when they happened, turned out horrible. I didn't know why. But that's the way it was. Dad did nothing but frustrate me.

When they bought the Belgrano house, I discovered I couldn't walk to Dad's any more. He was moving to another neighborhood and I told him I didn't like him being so far away. He answered that it wasn't that far. That it was only a twenty-minute bus ride. But I felt it was much more than twenty minutes. It seemed to me that Dad was getting further and further away. Going to his house was turning into more of an effort all the time.

Susana told me how they were arranging the new house. I would share a room with Inés, like in the place on Libertad. On the other hand, Luis and Pablo, who'd shared a room on Libertad, would each have his own room on Virrey Loreto. I felt my place in that family almost didn't exist anymore.

Everyone acted like we were a family. As if Luis and I were Susana's kids' brother and sister. I tried to believe it. I would have liked to have more brothers and sisters. But I knew it was a farce: Dad's house project just as much as the idea of us all being siblings. I always ended up feeling betrayed. There was no place for me. Whether or not they assigned me a bed, that was not my room. I was an intruder. I wandered around the house not knowing where to go. Believing Dad led straight to disappointment. And once again, the same old story: indifference reigned on Tuesdays and Thursdays at his place and on weekends in the country. Neglect. And that, supposedly, was a family.

Starting high school was awful for me. I didn't want to finish elementary school. I took the entrance exam for Liceo 5. I passed easily. I found it unpleasant that the school was girls-only. I didn't know why I'd chosen that school. Maybe because it was in Belgrano. Or because Pablo's girlfriend went there. The fact was, I couldn't stand going there every day.

In the first term, despite my indifference, I got good marks. I gave my report card to Mom for her to sign. In the little box where it said signature of parent, tutor or guardian, Mom, instead of signing it, wrote my name. She got mixed up. She came into my room in fits of laughter. She held out the report card so I could see. She'd written Luz Goldman. I laughed too although deep down I was thinking Mom was more despicable than ever. I tried to imagine what the prefect would say when I told her. It seemed unbelievable. This could only happen to Mom. I was scared the prefect would think I'd tried to forge my mom's signature. But I ruled that out; I'd have had to have been really crazy to mistakenly write my own name instead of hers. But it was suspicious to the school authorities in any case. They considered the report card a sacred document. What my mom had done struck them as absolute mockery.

The prefect listened, flabbergasted, to my anecdote. She found it hard to believe a mother would make such a mistake. She told me these things never happened. But now that it had occurred, my mom would have to apologize in writing to the principal. Mom wrote the letter. The next day I handed it in to the prefect. She looked at me indignantly. She shouted that you couldn't write a letter to the principal on that kind of paper. She said, "Official paper must be used!" Mom looked at me with a certain impatience. She had no idea about how to write a letter to the principal or what type of paper you should use. But if it was official paper she had to use, then I should go out and buy some. She wrote the letter again. This time they accepted it. I was furious with Mom. She didn't worry about the same things as other moms. In spite of everything, in some part of myself, I derived a certain pleasure: I liked that Mom showed no respect for authority. I didn't have to misbehave. She did it for me. And I laughed too.

That year—1977—Dad decided to leave the country. His plan was to set up house in New York with Susana, her four kids, Luis and me. At first, Susana didn't want to hear a word about leaving Buenos Aires. She and Dad argued a lot about it. But the situation in Argentina was getting steadily worse for Dad. He was constantly receiving anonymous death threats.

I was enthusiastic about the idea of leaving the country. I wanted to leave Mom. Luis had passed his final high school exams early so he had the year off. He liked the idea of going to college in the States. My friends said it was awful to leave Mom all alone. But to me Mom didn't matter. She'd let me down in every way. She'd even fallen out with Elena. It was unforgivable. Nothing she did was worthwhile. I was going with Dad and Susana.

I stopped going to school. In a few months I'd be in New York, why go to school here? I didn't even make a conscious decision to stop going. I just didn't go anymore. Nothing was said on the matter, not by Mom and not by Dad.

At the age of thirteen I didn't believe in anything. Absolutely nothing. I was a complete sceptic. I'd been betrayed in everything. I was left with no hopes that hadn't been frustrated, no dreams not disappointed. I didn't have my group of friends from elementary school anymore. I had nothing left in Buenos Aires. I had nothing left in life. I went to New York in the hope of forming a new family. With Dad, Susana and her kids. Susana, Dad, Andrés, José and I went together. Luis had gone ahead, on his own. Inés and Pablo were staying. Inés, to finish high school in December. Pablo, on the other hand, had another whole year to go. We left in August of 1977.

The Sunday of our departure, Mom came to wake me up. She said we'd say goodbye then. That later it would be worse. That she didn't want to come with me to Ezeiza. It would be too sad. I said okay. If she didn't want to come with me she didn't have to. It didn't matter to me. It didn't seem like I was leaving. Everything was foggy. The night before, Mom and I had gone to see a movie. We saw Bergman's *Magic Flute*. I knew Dad, Susana and some of her kids were also there but we didn't run into each other. I wasn't taking very much. I felt like I didn't have anything. I packed some clothes and a few trinkets. That last Sunday in Buenos Aires, we went out for lunch: Susana, her kids, Dad and I. Susana showed me a bracelet her best friend Violeta had given her. She told me how they'd parted, I remembered how I'd left Mom. I'd said goodbye to her with my mind completely blank. Without thinking anything. Nothing mattered to me. I didn't cry. I didn't feel sad. I didn't feel hatred. I didn't feel anything.

VI

Nothing could be worse than a visit from my grandmother. She arrived in Bronxville one morning in March, the day after Pablo left. I didn't want to go meet her at the airport: Daddy and Susana went.

Living in the Bronxville house were: Dad, Susana, Andrés, Inés, José and I. Leo, Inés's boyfriend, had lived with us for a few months. Then he and Luis rented an apartment in the Village together. Luis had lived with us for a while too; but he had a fight with Susana and left.

Luis and Susana had always hated each other. Susana loathed him. She blamed him for everything. She was cruel and unfair to him. I hated her for that. But I hated Dad more. He didn't know how to defend what belonged to him: his son. I didn't say anything. I preferred not to get involved. I was afraid Susana would hate me too. In reality, it was obvious we couldn't stand each other, but we never had confrontations.

Pablo was the only one of Susana's kids who lived in Buenos Aires. He was in high school. He'd come to New York for the summer holidays. In March he went back to Buenos Aires for the start of term. When Pablo left I felt like I'd lost my soul. I adored Luis and Pablo. I got along really well with both of them; they'd both gone. And now my grandmother Gimena was coming. What a nightmare!

Around that time I found out that Inés was definitely staying to live with "us." How infuriating! Having to share my room again! And they didn't even have the decency to tell me. No, they installed her in my room overnight. They brought another bed and that was it. Sort yourselves out! She filled my closet with her clothes. Stuck whatever she wanted all over the walls and I wasn't allowed to say a single word. Worst of all, Susana would come in at night to chat with Inés and they'd practically whisper so I couldn't hear what they were saying.

Gimena's visit was torture. Susana couldn't stand her. She treated her like garbage. She went on for hours saying horrible things about her, sounding like a broken record. She criticized her cooking, the way she spoke, said Gimena had no interest in museums and only went to them so she could show off to her acquaintances back in Buenos Aires. Whenever Gimena said anything, Susana smiled ironically. I couldn't bear the level of tension we'd reached since my grandmother had been there. Dad and Gimena had never gotten along. Not that they'd ever fallen out. They didn't even argue. They upheld a formal mother-son relationship. I suppose it must have bothered Dad that Susana said such nasty things about his mother, but he never said anything.

I was sleeping when someone came to tell me that Gimena had arrived. I never called her grandma or granny or any of those things. I called all my relatives by their names. No titles, except for Mom and Dad. She was Gimena, or "Dad's mom." Ever since I could remember she was so old, ready to die at any moment, and in spite of that, at eighty she seemed to have years left. When I heard she was there, I didn't even feel like going to say hello. It seemed horrible that Pablo had gone and the very next day Gimena came. I was getting fed up with living in New York.

Bronxville was on the outskirts, half an hour from Manhattan; it was an upscale suburb. I was used to living downtown. At first I liked the idea of living in a house: later it turned out to be unbearable. A week after my grandmother's arrival, there was a school holiday. The day before I went into Manhattan. I'd arranged to spend the day off shopping for clothes with Susana. Since I was already in Manhattan, I decided to sleep over at Luis's place. I asked him if it was okay. He said yeah. That he had plans to go out and Leo wouldn't be home either, but I could stay there anyway.

I went to his house. I wondered what to do until I was ready to go to bed. I did the usual, listened to music at full volume through headphones. That way I couldn't hear anything else and I couldn't talk. Even though I was alone in Luis's apartment at the time, I put these enormous headphones on anyway.

Someone came to say hello. It was Leo, he took me completely by surprise. I told him I was staying overnight and that Luis had told me that neither of them would be there. Leo didn't pay much attention. He started talking to me as if I were grown up. I was fourteen years old and he was twenty-three. He'd been going out with Inés for two years. They were "the couple." Leo had always seemed unattainable to me. That night we were alone in an apartment where we were both going to sleep. Leo didn't stop talking and I understood less and less of what was going on. It seemed really strange for him to be so interested in talking to me. He asked me what I was planning to do that night. I told him I didn't have any plans, that I was just sleeping over there because I didn't have school the next day. He asked me if I wanted to go with him to a street called St. Mark's Place. It was cool, the places there stayed open until two or three in the morning, it was full of punks. He told me there were nice vests on sale, and he also mentioned Patti Smith, a punk singer. I liked her and had been to see her at a new club—the C.B.G.B.—where all the punk groups played. He also talked to me about some people from a medical institute where he worked. In some way I didn't immediately understand, they were all connected: him, Patti Smith, and the ones from the institute. They got money together and bought marijuana off the same person. I told him I didn't feel like going out for a walk. He decided to go on his own, but he didn't end up going, we kept talking. Leo was not at all conventional. I found him sort of repulsive but at the same time I liked him. I liked him because he was Inés's boyfriend; and Inés didn't know that we two were alone that night. Yes, the two of us alone, without Inés. Maybe Inés would hate me if she found out. I didn't care anymore.

We didn't have anything more to talk about. I decided to go to bed. Before I'd fallen asleep, Leo called me from his room. He said there was something good on TV, a program about The Beatles. I got up and went to his room. I was surprised to see the television wasn't on. I didn't say anything. I tried to act as if this were the most normal situation in the world. I was a virgin, I'd never felt so close to going to bed with someone before. It was overwhelming, my wish come true: Leo wanted something from me and Inés wouldn't find out. I could have revenge, my revenge for everything she'd made me suffer. She'd stolen my dad and now I was stealing her boyfriend. Leo liked me better, in reality he preferred me, he didn't love her. Leo said there was a bed in his room, I could sleep there. However, before I even realized it myself, I answered no and went to sleep in my brother's room, with the feeling that something indescribable had just happened.

My thoughts overwhelmed me, I didn't understand any of what was going on. I couldn't figure out if this was all real or if I was imagining it. What would Dad say if I told him? He probably wouldn't have believed me, he would have said I was a liar, that it couldn't be true that I could catch Leo's attention. That Inés was pretty but I wasn't. That I should stop making up stories.

I fell asleep completely confused. We didn't even kiss. A kiss would have been enough to have me walking on air. A kiss. What would I have felt? No, it wouldn't have been me. I fell asleep immediately on the mattress I'd prepared in Luis's room, without even turning down the sheets.

The next morning I woke up with a very strange feeling in my whole body. I looked at my hands, they were really swollen, so swollen I could barely close them. I was looking at my hands and I didn't recognize them. And my feet! They were so swollen my shoes almost didn't fit.

I'd turned into a monster; that wasn't me. The night before someone else had gotten into bed instead of me. I felt disgusting, itchy. I had enormous red blotches all over my body and the sensation of never having been so dirty. I ran to take a shower. I looked in Leo's room, he'd already gone out. Although I took a long shower, it didn't help at all. I felt just as dirty. After much effort, I managed to get my shoes on. The blotches were getting bigger. It seemed like an unstoppable rash, I couldn't think of any way to keep it from spreading. I wished, I pleaded to return to my normal state which, much as I disliked it, was much better than this. I was shocked by my face in the mirror. I couldn't go outside looking like that. Much less, shopping for clothes.

Susana and I had arranged to meet in the doorway of a store that very afternoon. It was my chance to buy clothes. At first I didn't know how to convince Daddy and Susana I needed new clothes. It didn't even occur to me that Susana would be seeking my complicity against her mother-in-law. I'd been wearing the same jeans for months, maybe it was that. We were going specifically to buy pants. That time was special. Just Susana and I were going. Yes, Susana was going to dedicate a little of her precious time to taking me shopping.

The shopping centers were a long way from home. You could only get there by car. They always promised we could go buy clothes on Saturday afternoons. But it took ages. There were so many of us. So if someone was going to buy one nail, everyone wanted to go. By the time we managed to leave it was mid-afternoon. There wasn't much time left. The library was on the way and someone always had books to return. We'd go there first. The library was more important than anything else. I never took books out of the library. I wasn't interested in anything they had. More than that, I hated all library books. Inés, on the other hand, was much better than me. She always found something interesting. Dad and Susana spent hours inside that place. At first, I'd wait for them in the car. I thought they'd just take back the books and that would be that. Silly me! They looked at every single book. I thought if I waited in the car they'd hurry.

They never hurried. When I saw how late it was and realized the stores would be closing soon, I'd get out of the car and, trying to contain my fury, go and ask them to please hurry. They'd say, yes, they were coming in just a minute. Don't nag. Have some patience. I couldn't stand it for a half a second longer. I hated that damned library more and more intensely. My despair was so great that I began to feel a twitching in my legs, an uncontrollable physical reaction. I swore I'd never set foot in that place again. That if it meant going to that filthy library first, I didn't even care about clothes anymore. They could stick it.

That school holiday, for some strange reason, Susana and I were going together, just the two of us, to one of the nicest stores in New York. I looked like a monster. There was no way I was going to tell Susana that Leo had asked me to go out the night before.

In the afternoon, I met Susana in front of the entrance to the store. She noticed I had blotches on my face. I told her I'd woken up like that. I was quite a bit less swollen by then, though I was still having the allergic reaction. Susana bought me a pair of pants.

In the evening, on the train home, I started coming out in enormous blotches again. I thought of Inés. I looked at my arm and felt like throwing up. The blotches were red, huge and quickly multiplying. It was impossible to stop the rash spreading. I was practically immobilized. I just wanted to get home, go to bed, and not talk to anyone.

Dad and Susana never believed we were sick. They had to be convinced and even then they didn't worry. Getting sick was a bum deal. When I was sick, I missed Mom and Ester so much. They certainly took care of me. They made me special meals and brought them to me in bed. They called the doctor and stayed by my bedside. I felt cared for, protected. Mom had her faults but she was my mom.

In contrast, getting sick at Dad's was the worst. I felt more abandoned than ever. To get food brought to me in bed I would have had to be on the verge of death, and even then they wouldn't have brought anything good.

They paid no attention to my allergy even though I was practically deformed. When they saw I couldn't get out of bed, they decided to call the doctor. He prescribed some pills over the phone. He told them to be careful because they caused severe drowsiness. I didn't manage to find out if the pills were a cure for the allergy or just knocked you out so you didn't notice anything. I was in a state of semiconsciousness for a couple of days. When I woke up, I broke out again.

The next day I went to my dance lesson. While I was there the blotches started to come out again. The teacher suggested I go home. I went to get changed and called Dad. I asked him to come and pick me up. Dad came with Susana. She told me off, saying I hadn't taken all the pills I was supposed to. I thought it must be true, now that I was awake, but I denied it. I told her I had taken all the pills. Maybe I was lying. It seemed to me I'd actually taken one less. Or maybe not. Maybe I was telling the truth. I didn't care. I generally lied. It wouldn't have been strange if I was lying that time too. Susana asked me how many pills I'd taken. She looked at the strip and counted how many were gone. She said I was lying to her: there was one more than what I said. She shouted that if I kept this up I'd never get over this allergy. They were both angry with me. They swore that, from then on, I'd have to take all the pills. I wanted them to take care of me. I felt even worse when they got mad at me. I wanted them to be especially nice to me and they were especially mean. No one understood what was happening to me. My feeling was that I couldn't take any more. Susana arrived at the conclusion that my allergy was a result of the presence of Gimena in the house. She thought it was funny. She said I was allergic to my grandmother. I hadn't thought of that and I believed Susana was right. That my grand-mother's being there had caused that rash all over my body.

VII

My stay in New York ended at the age of fourteen. A couple of days after I got back to Buenos Aires, Pablo phoned. Luis answered. Pablo asked him if he was staying home. Luis answered no, he was going out with Malena. My brother Luis's girlfriend was in Buenos Aires even though he lived in New York. Pablo wanted to talk to me. He asked me if I was staying in. I said yes. He said he was coming over for a visit. I thought it was strange, Pablo never came over to see me. I tried to hide my surprise and told him I'd be expecting him. Mom wouldn't be home that night either. She was going out with her boyfriend who lived with us practically all the time but never got around to clarifying the situation.

I realized I was waiting anxiously for Pablo. I had this fantasy that when he arrived he was going to kiss me on the lips.

As soon as Mom and her boyfriend left, Pablo arrived. We said hello as usual, with a kiss on the cheek. We went to Luis's room. We started talking. Pablo was acting strange, really strange. He told me he'd taken quaaludes. First it was one, then several. While we were talking, he came closer. "You look pretty." I was thrilled to hear him say it. He tried to take my hand. I pulled it away, not really meaning it. He took a joint out of his pocket. "I want to smoke." I said no. Not to. That I didn't want Mom to smell it. But Pablo didn't pay any attention to me. He wanted to smoke it no matter what. I grabbed it out of his hand. We broke it. Two pieces fell on the floor. Pablo laughed.

Pablo couldn't control his movements by then. I couldn't figure out if he was aware of what he was doing or not. He said he wanted to kiss me. I shouted that he couldn't. He insisted. He came over and I ran away. He tripped over a chair and fell on the floor. "You're a jerk," I said. He got mad. He asked me not to call him anything like that again. He was offended. I apologized, "It just slipped out." I felt even more scared, realizing that Pablo was aware of what he was doing. I was alarmed at the possibility that Mom might come home and see him in that state.

Pablo went to the bathroom. He took a long time so I decided to see what was going on. I found him leaning over the sink with his pants all wet. I thought he'd pissed himself. I realized he hadn't; he'd tried to take another quaalude. Since he didn't have a glass, the water ran all over him. I told him he shouldn't take another. I tried to get them out of his hands. He pulled hard and so did I. I finally managed to convince him and we went back to the room.

I didn't know what to do. It worried me to see him like that. It made me mad that he was in such a state. But I was attracted to him. I doubted he really thought I was pretty: he was so out of it. I tried to get Pablo to keep still, he could barely walk by then but he kept staggering back and forth.

Luis and Malena came back. I told them Pablo was in rough shape and would have to be taken home. Pablo wanted to go on his own. He wouldn't let anyone come with him. We tried to convince him. He was furious that we didn't believe him. Finally, Pablo let Luis and Malena go with him.

On the one hand, I was very relieved when Pablo left, but on the other, I hadn't wanted them to take him. That night Pablo was mine. He liked me and I liked him too. I would have liked him to stay with me forever, even if it were like that, even if he bumped into the furniture and could barely talk.

When he got back home, Luis told me how it had all gone. They couldn't get a taxi driver to agree to take Pablo. They had no choice but to walk with Pablo draped over their shoulders. Malena held him up on one side and Luis on the other.

Pablo lived with his dad and his dad's wife in a house in Palermo Chico, some twenty blocks from our apartment.

Luis told me that at every curb, they had to lift him. "But then came the worst," said Luis. He didn't remember which house was Pablo's and neither did Pablo. No matter how hard they tried to get Pablo to remember, they couldn't. Suddenly, Pablo pointed to a house. "It's that one." The three of them went up to it. Pablo went in. Luis and Malena stayed in the doorway. After a while, Luis went in too. He saw Pablo coming down the stairs saying no, this wasn't his house. Luis couldn't understand. They were in some stranger's house and the maid had let them in. The woman who lived there took it all calmly and informed Luis, "That boy's on drugs." Luis added that Pablo didn't remember where he lived. "Incredible," I thought. We figured it was pretty lucky the woman hadn't called the police.

They finally found Pablo's house. They left him there. Pablo was unconscious by then.

I couldn't tell him about Pablo wanting to kiss me. Anyhow, what did it matter.

VIII

The last months of my time in New York had been dismal. I turned fourteen in November. When spring came, I started feeling worse than ever. I had no friends at school and didn't know what to do about my life. I felt bad, really bad.

At the beginning of June I had my final exams. The day I came home from my math exam Dad and Susana were furious. They'd found a little box of marijuana in my room. I told them it couldn't be true and, if it had been there, someone must have put it there. But it had a little label with my name on it, there was no doubt it was mine. Although I tried to lie to them, it was impossible. It was all too obvious. Dad opened the little box in front of me and flushed its contents down the toilet. Dad and Susana were really angry with me. I didn't care. I didn't care about anything in the world.

When school finished I felt lonelier than ever. I hated Dad's house, I hated everyone. Summer depressed me, worried me. I preferred winter, I'd rather it were five degrees below zero. That made me happy: I was going to the winter, I was going to Argentina.

At the time, Argentina was in the midst of the Soccer World Cup. It was 1978. I didn't understand what it was about. Dad and Susana said it was all a sham. We found out through the letters we got from Argentina that the most chic women were spending hours getting made up at the hairdresser's in order to go to the soccer stadium and that whenever Argentina won a match, huge crowds gathered at the Obelisk to celebrate. But that people without much money couldn't afford to go to the grounds. The tickets were exorbitant. Apparently, the traditional reputation of the Colón Theatre as the most elegant place to be seen in Buenos Aires had been forgotten. The most distinguished place was the soccer stadium. However, in La Boca, the most seriously fanatical soccer neighborhood, nothing happened. It was all quiet. They didn't celebrate the World Cup victories there.

We spent the last days in New York going back and forth from the immigration office home and from home back to the immigration office. They were on the verge of granting us green cards but the paperwork took ages. Dad got really nervous. He said we couldn't leave the United States until we got our green cards. I trembled when I heard that. I didn't give a shit about the green card. I wanted to go to Buenos Aires. Luis had gone to Buenos Aires in the middle of June. Dad, Susana and Inés were staying in New York all summer. Andrés and José were flying with me.

A few hours before leaving for the airport, I just didn't know what to do with myself. I couldn't endure another second. I thought maybe I'd roll a joint with some little leaves off a plant I'd grown and dried myself. I went to smoke it in the guest room so it wouldn't smell up my room. Susana came upstairs to ask me for the iron and smelled the pot. She went straight to tell Dad. Inés told me to put it out, that you could smell it all over the house. Go to hell, I thought.

Dad and Susana appeared. They told me not to smoke anymore. I told them I wasn't smoking anything. Susana looked at me with hatred. "You're a liar." Dad agonized. He didn't want to tell me off just then. Susana did. She wanted to tell me off. She was always finding some excuse to tell me I was rotten. Later I thought that really, I could have gone outside and smoked it walking around the block. But it was done now, they'd already told me off.

I'd just read *The Catcher in the Rye* for the second time. It was one of the few things I could get enthusiastic about. I used to spend hours lying on my bed pulling apart my split ends. My hair was pretty long. I didn't want to cut it. Anyway, no one noticed the messiness of my hair.

I got to Buenos Aires a week after the World Cup finished. It seemed like the only thing anyone talked about. I hadn't seen Mom or Ester for a whole year. I'd sent letters with Luis to give to Mara and Laura, my two best friends. Mommy and Luis came to meet me at the airport. Luis told me that Mom asked him, "Is that her with the long hair?" They told me they had a room all ready for me. It had been Ester's room; she lived with her husband now. Luis still had his room, the same as ever. Mom was in my room. The one that'd been hers had been transformed into her office. She gave her English classes there. Luis had painted my new room. He decorated it with excellent posters. I thought it was an ideal room for fucking.

I was glad to see Ester again. I found my friends were a bit of a mess. Laura told me she wasn't really friends with Mara anymore. They only saw each other at school. They never went out together. I got along pretty well with Mara at first, but then I didn't feel like seeing her anymore.

Luis, Mom, sometimes her boyfriend and I were living together. Mom was worried because she found out Luis and I smoked marijuana. We tried to convince her that it was completely normal in the States, that it was nothing to worry about. For Mom it was serious. And we weren't getting along at all. We did nothing but argue. I got along well with Luis, we were very close, united against Mom. We thought she was a retard.

Malena, Luis's girlfriend, lived in Buenos Aires. He and Mom were always fighting because he wanted to sleep with his girlfriend at home. Mom wouldn't let him. The atmosphere at home was hell. Luis and I had nothing to do. It was the middle of the school year for our friends. I was almost never at home. I spent every afternoon with Laura, at her place.

For the winter holidays, Mom, Luis, Malena and I went to Punta del Este. It was awful. Mom and Luis didn't stop fighting for a single second. Always the same old story. Luis wanted Malena to sleep in the same room as him. Mom wouldn't let them. They were unbearable. I couldn't stand it anymore.

When we got back to Buenos Aires, Mom suggested we get family therapy. We laughed. We didn't want anything to do with any therapy. But she nagged on about it so much that we eventually agreed. The three of us went to a psychoanalyst.

It was something new to me. I didn't open my mouth. I didn't say a single word. Mom and Luis talked the whole time during that first session. I wasn't interested in fighting or arguing. It didn't seem to be worth saying anything.

The psychoanalyst said, "Luz's silence speaks volumes." But at home that had never been of any interest. In spite of not speaking, I took hope from the therapy session. I liked the analyst even though, at the same time, I hated him for the things he said to me. He told Luis and me we needed to undergo analysis whether in Buenos Aires or in the States. He assured me of my propensity towards drug addiction and possibly getting involved with a psychopath. It scared me a lot. I started to have doubts about my return to New York. To feel I didn't want to live at Dad's house anymore. I discovered, much to my surprise, that I wanted to stay with Mom in Buenos Aires. Luis felt like staying in Buenos Aires too. Even though he fought with Mom, he realized he was better off with her as well. How to tell Dad all this? It was a betrayal. Dad would hate me. I phoned him. I told him about my misgivings. My parents had an arrangement by which Luis and I could choose where we wanted to live. So I was the one who had to decide. No one would do it for me. Dad repeated this to me. I hated my parents. How could they be so cruel? Deep down, we didn't matter to either of them and, still, they tugged at us. Mom, availing herself of all the future advantages that, from what she said, we'd get from living with her. Dad, assuring us that living with him was best. And, of course, the opportunities offered by New York went without saying. He wasn't even going to bother comparing it to this fucking city with its seemingly eternal military dictatorship. The military regime and the opportunities I could have in New York didn't matter to me. I just wanted them to care about me, wherever; to stop tugging at me. I felt like cutting myself in half, giving one piece to Mom and the other to Dad. I didn't know what to do. Something, deep down, told me it was better for me to stay with Mom. I knew, in that case, I'd lose Dad for good. He wouldn't forgive such a betrayal. Forcing me to chose between my mom and my dad was the worst. In reality, I knew it all boiled down to a dispute between them. They fought over us as if we were toys. Why? Why did they do that? Whatever decision I made was a punishment. A terrible punishment. Whoever I decided in favor of, I knew the other would hate me. My life was torture.

Dad preferred not to come to Argentina due to the political situation. In '66, during the "night of the long knives," he had been fired, along with most of his colleagues, from a tenured professorship in the Faculty of Sciences. In '69, for taking part in a general strike, he was dismissed from his post as director of the Institute of Radio Astronomy. In '74, he applied for a position teaching physics in the Faculty of Engineering and was turned down on the grounds that he was too gifted to hold that chair. In '75, the "Triple A" had come looking for him. After all that, the memory of Argentina caused Dad terrible pain. He didn't want to come. So Susana would be coming. She would be Dad's representative. I didn't want her to come: I wanted them to leave me alone. Not to pressure me anymore. To let me get on with my life. Stop threatening me. I felt like a delinquent. Nobody understood me, nobody paid me any attention. But when it came to deciding where I was going to live, there was no letup.

The night before Susana's arrival, I locked myself in my room to write. Without stopping, I wrote everything I was feeling: that I hated my parents, and Susana, and the family therapist who'd been wrong to tell me I could get hooked on drugs. He shouldn't have told me those things: now it was sure to happen. When we got to New York in 1977 Susana had forbidden us to smoke marijuana. It was the first thing I did. I wanted to vanish off the face of the earth. I couldn't stand for anyone to come near me. Ester was the only one who didn't pressure me.

With her, in Buenos Aires, I felt at home. With Laura too, and Luis. But not with anyone else. Luis protected me and I did the same for him. Our therapist had said that I mothered him and he was a father figure to me. We'd been like that our whole lives. We took care of each other. For me, Luis was one of the most important people in the world. He was the only one who'd never abandoned me. We were completely loyal to each other. We were as one. I always took him into account. But that night, when I wrote till I exhausted myself, I couldn't bear to have anyone around, not even my brother.

I wrote in a notebook that Susana had given me as a present before I left New York. I felt guilty for using that notebook to shit on them all. My head pounded. I wrote without stopping. My headache got steadily worse. Until I couldn't keep writing and fell asleep.

The next day Luis went to see Susana. She was staying at her mother's. He told me she was really nice to him. That she'd been kind. That when he left she'd seen him to the door. His comment about seeing him to the door bothered me. I told myself it was nothing out of the ordinary, though it had certainly made an impression on him.

A couple of days later, I went to see Susana. I couldn't get up the nerve to broach the subject of my uncertainty about where to live. Susana was really angry with Violeta, her best friend. She'd found out that Violeta had been the first one to give her son Pablo marijuana. When Dad and Susana lived in Buenos Aires, Violeta was Susana's best friend in the world: witty, vivacious and fabulous. I couldn't stand her. She used to come to our place in the country every weekend. She'd bring her faggot friends who were mean to me and my friends. They bossed us around. Every so often they'd ask us if we'd seen the matches. They'd take them. Later they'd come back and ask us again where the matches were. They'd order us to look for them. Dad couldn't stand Violeta's faggot friends. But Susana thought they were really funny. Lulo Gallo was her favorite.

Now, seeing Susana's rage, I understood why Violeta's faggot friends were always so desperate for matches. As far as Susana was concerned, Violeta had gone crazy. Rotten. Susana had decided to go on an anti-drugs crusade. Right there in her mother's living room, I listened to her having an argument, over the phone, with a guy who sold drugs to Pablo. She was trying to get him to agree to get together with her for a chat or something ludicrous like that. I was shocked that Susana seemed to think that seeing her son for a few days in Buenos Aires would be enough to fix up his life. She was convinced of it. She sent him to a psychoanalyst and thought that was all fixed up. She went back to New York satisfied. Sure of having fulfilled her maternal duties.

It was becoming increasingly clear to me that I couldn't go back to living with Dad and Susana. That was worse than hell. My vacation would soon be over. My supposed return to New York was getting closer. I summoned up courage and told Susana over the phone that I wasn't going back. "You're crazy, completely crazy, you're coming back with me and that's all there is to it!" Mom butted into the conversation to defend me. All three of us were on the line. Mom told Susana I would do whatever I wanted. I listened to all that and wanted to die. Both of them shouted. But on top of that, everyone was shouting all the time and everywhere. Doors slammed. I locked myself in my room and hated them. Susana demanded that I come over and speak to her in person. Mom wanted to come with me. She said all three of us needed to talk. I begged her not to come, please, no. It would be crazy and I screamed that I couldn't take any more.

Dad phoned. He said Susana had told him of my decision. "You have to come back, it's already all arranged." He added that, if I wanted to stay in Buenos Aires, I should at least come back to New York first and talk it over with him and then, if I still wanted to, I could go back.

I couldn't do that. I didn't feel up to taking a plane, talking to Dad, spending a week in New York and coming back. I was sure that I didn't matter to Dad. His request was nothing more than a question of pride.

Susana renewed her campaign by telling me how they were thinking of moving into Manhattan and buying a house for the weekends. She knew how much I'd wanted that, but I didn't believe them. We'd had weekend houses before, a house in Buenos Aires, a place in Lujan, a house in Bronxville. It had always been the same. Change houses though they might, they remained the same. I wasn't jumping on that bandwagon again. I'd had too bad a time living with them. They had a real smart facade, really winning. But I wasn't buying it anymore.

Mom asked me to stay in Buenos Aires. She said she'd pay for me to have therapy, that she'd fix up my room and take care of me. Mom didn't want Luis and me to go back to New York.

I went to talk to Susana. I told her my mind was made up: I was staying with Mom. She warned me that Dad would be very angry. I told her, unexpectedly, that I loved her. In reality, I didn't know if it were true. I didn't know what I felt. But I didn't want them to hate me anymore. I didn't want them to tell me off anymore. I hugged her. She gave me a book of poetry. It was by her. She signed it: "For Luz, in your search for your own way, with much love from Susana. Buenos Aires. September 2nd, 1978." I didn't believe her. I knew I was losing them. I had chosen Mom. They would never forgive me.

José and Andrés were going back to New York with her. Luis didn't know what to do. He said Susana had come down to rustle kids from Buenos Aires. So that none would think of staying. But I was staying. I was the black sheep.

Classes were about to start in New York. Luis had to decide what to do. He was in Buenos Aires with his girlfriend. He really wanted to stay. But he didn't. He couldn't get up the nerve to defy Dad. He decided to go back to New York. I'd had a feeling that was going to happen. Staying with Mom didn't just mean losing Dad, but Luis too.

We took him to Ezeiza. When Mom and I got home, I went to his room. I bawled my eyes out. I felt like I was going to die. I felt a profound emptiness. A part of me had gone with Luis. The only person who'd stood by me had been dragged away. I put on a Spinetta record, a song that went: "Take good care of the child, take care of his mind. Keep him off drugs, never repress him...." Luis didn't know when he'd be able to come back. He had to save money. Before he left, I'd stuck a note and a little ceramic piggy bank I'd had for ages into his suitcase. That day I felt like I'd lost my soul. I no longer had a dad. I no longer had a brother. We'd probably never even live in the same country ever again.

IX

At noon one day I ran into Mara on the bus. We hadn't seen each other for a few months. I was just on my way to have lunch with my grandmother. At first we looked at each other somewhat suspiciously, but pretty soon the friendship we'd always had won out. We arranged that as soon as lunch was finished, I'd go over to her place.

I told Mara I was going out with Raúl. She was going out with a guy I didn't know. We were fifteen. The only subject we were interested in was who had fucked and who hadn't. I had, I'd fucked by then.

Mara came over to my place on Saturday. She announced that she was sleeping over. The plan was to go over to Laura's that night. We went early. Pablo and his girlfriend came over later. Pablo had become really good friends with Raúl. Mara and I were in our third year of high school, Raúl was in fourth and Pablo was in his first year of law school. But we weren't the slightest bit interested in our education.

Mara had always liked Pablo. Me too. I was really glad Pablo and Raúl were friends. That way I had Pablo around. But at the same time he bugged me: he took Raúl away from me. They adored each other. Pablo spent every afternoon at Raúl's. I was convinced Raúl liked him more than he liked me.

As usual, at a certain point in the evening, Pablo and Raúl had to go out to make a deal. We spent the whole time smoking marijuana. Sometimes we did cocaine too. I hadn't tried any other drugs. They had, they'd done everything. Especially Raúl. The year before, he'd done nothing but shoot up. In October he ended up in jail with a bunch of his friends. He was in there for twenty days. When he got out he decided to stop shooting up.

I didn't know if I loved Raúl or not. At times, I couldn't stand him; I got fed up with his stories about jail and drugs. That night they'd arranged to get some speed.

Laura's parents had gone out. Tons of people came over. We were smoking and everything seemed funny. Laura's brother tried to impose some order: he didn't want any more people coming in. "If you keep shouting, the neighbors are going to call the cops!" Since nobody paid him any attention he decided we all had to leave, no exceptions. Nobody seemed to hear him. He appeared with a rifle and pointed it at us. His eyes were popping out of his head. Even so, we kept smoking and laughing. "Fucking bastards! Get out of here or I'll blow your fucking heads off!" Someone turned the music off and I found myself caught in an avalanche of people running for the door. Laura's brother kept shouting his head off and we could still hear him from the street.

A bunch of girls and Mara's boyfriend ended up at my apartment. We were waiting for Pablo and Raúl to come back from getting the stuff.

We heard the back doorbell ring. I went to see who it was. Through the glass, even though it was dark, I could see it was a policeman. I ran back to the living room and shouted: "Shit, you guys, it's the cops!" Sandra and Mara grabbed their purses and went to the front door. They didn't go out: they thought it would look suspicious, although in reality, we hadn't done anything wrong. Meanwhile, another girl peeked out the door and shouted that it wasn't a cop, it was Pablo. I knew I hadn't been seeing things. It would be pretty difficult for me to confuse Pablo with a cop. Anyway, since I didn't have a key for the back door, I was going to have to ask whoever it was to come around to the main door. When I looked out, I confirmed my first impression: there was a policeman standing there.

It was about three in the morning. Mom wasn't home. The policeman came in. We stood around him. Mute. He asked whose house it was. I answered that it was mine. He wanted to know who was the girlfriend of one of the boys who were downstairs. Again I answered that it was me. He asked us a few questions about our occupations and not much else. Then he left, just the way he'd arrived.

When Pablo and Raúl came in they told us they'd been stopped by a patrol car. They were on the comer outside Laura's place. Even though all their ID was in order, the police asked where they were going and insisted on going with them.

After a while everyone except Mara left. I thought it was strange that Mom hadn't come home yet. Raúl was at his house with Pablo. They phoned to invite Mara and me to come over there. We agreed. I put in my diaphragm while I was chatting with Mara. I said I didn't know if we'd fuck or not but I'd have it in just in case. Having sex with Raúl didn't give me any pleasure. In fact, it hurt quite a bit. Neither Raúl nor I understood what we were feeling ourselves, much less what was going on with the other person. I'd never even had an orgasm. I wondered what everyone else thought was so great about making love. Raúl didn't get it either. For him, fucking was just like masturbating.

The four of us were together in Raúl's room until dawn. Raúl and I in the bed. Pablo and Mara, crashed out on pillows on the floor. Pablo and Mara became a couple.

X

It was a few days before Christmas. Mara and I had finished our third year of high school. Raúl had finished his fourth but had to take exams in every subject. Pablo had dropped out of college and been on vacation for eight months; in March he'd start his military service.

Since I'd passed every subject already, I didn't have any exams and I was totally bored all through December. Classes finished at the end of November and I had nothing to do until March. For Raúl, on the other hand, December and February were his busiest months. He spent them studying for his exams. He did it willingly. But at the end of December he stopped studying until February. We confronted the holidays.

For several months, Pablo, Raúl, Mara and I had been spending all our time together. Always the four of us. Raúl's house was perfect for hanging out together. It was so big that his parents didn't even see us. They never asked us what we were doing. They didn't hear the records we played either. Raúl had the mezzanine. We'd lie on Raúl's bed smoking pot. We practically lived in that room, with the music turned up full blast or the television on. With all the smoke from the pot, cigarettes, incense and whatever else we tried to get to mask the smell of the marijuana, it was almost impossible to breathe. The room only had one window. It was normally closed. We didn't like to let too much light in. Although Raúl's house was practically a mansion, his room was more like a kennel. Actually, it was one: the dog was always in there. We'd baptized Raúl's room doubly: "the lair" or "the hovel."

Mara would phone me as soon as she got home from school. She said she'd rather speak to me before Pablo. For that matter, Pablo and Raúl also talked on the phone. As soon as

Raúl got back from school, Pablo went over to his house. Then they'd call us up.

Halfway through December, Pablo went to New York. His absence scared me. In a way, he protected me. He took my side and he calmed Mara down. He was like a buffer between me and Mara. Without Pablo in the middle, we were running a risk. Raúl had been left with me and Mara. I was sure that while Pablo was away, something would happen between Mara and Raúl. While on the one hand it made me furious watching how Mara was seducing Raúl, on the other, I wanted it. I said to Raúl that Mara was pretty. He thought so too. But I was certain that he liked Pablo more than Mara.

Mara was always phoning me. I felt important. Still, sometimes I couldn't stand her and wanted her out of the way. But no. Being alone with Raúl frightened me. Mara, Raúl and I were an inseparable trio. Till death do us part.

Once I had to leave them alone together. I would have preferred not to. I knew perfectly well what would happen between him and Mara. When I got back to Raúl's house I asked them what they'd been doing. Mara knew what I was getting at and looked at me out of the corner of her eye. "What've we been doing? Raúl showed me his new clothes." I hated them. I shouldn't have left them alone. But the situation was out of my hands. There was nothing I could do to change it.

Gerardo, a guy we knew, was about to go to Paraguay to buy some drugs. We thought we'd put in an order: half a pound of grass. We planned to leave it in Buenos Aires for the summer, ready for when we got back from vacation.

Mom and I were going to Punta del Este on the twenty-third of December and Raúl the following day. Mara was going to the States for a month with her parents and two sisters: a few days skiing in Colorado and the rest of the time in New York. My plan was to stay in Punta del Este until the first week of January, go back to Buenos Aires and then go to Europe on my own for the rest of January. First I'd join my brother Luis in

Rome. In February I was going to New York, where Mara, Pablo and I would all get together again.

Raúl wanted to go to New York. I had asked Dad if we could both come to his house. He said no. No way. I got really mad at Dad, even though in a way, it was a relief. I was sick of spending all day every day with Raúl. And the idea of having sex in Dad's house was inconceivable. Daddy and Luis were in New York. What did I need Raúl for? Pablo was there too and I wanted him to myself. Mara was no obstacle. I had no problem sharing him with her. It was Raúl who was my rival. He had qualities I could never match.

The day before Christmas, Gerardo was supposed to get back to Buenos Aires. I was never concerned with the deals. I didn't worry about making them or putting money in. Mara did. She was always on top of it all. Raúl was constantly on the phone trying to find out if Gerardo was back. He was told he'd be back soon. If not today then tomorrow. I went to Punta del Este and we still hadn't heard anything from Gerardo.

The first night in Punta del Este, I ran into a bunch of people I knew. We went out dancing. I was dancing with a guy who I thought was cute. But the only possible man in my life was Raúl. I'd only had sex with him. Although I sometimes found Raúl repulsive, I couldn't imagine being anyone else's girlfriend.

Before we started going out, Raúl had had some homo-sexual experiences. We tried, on the one hand, not to talk about it. We knew it was distressing for Raúl and, indirectly, for me as well. But on the other hand, curiosity made me ask, made me want to know the most sordid details. Yeah, I wanted to find out about the details. It gave me a certain pleasure. Then I'd call him a fucking faggot. I'd throw it right back in his face. Make him feel bad. Make him feel like trash. I'd hound him about not being a real man. But, at the same time, I liked the fact that he was like that. I thought it would be impossible to be with a guy who only wanted to fuck women. Raúl wanted everything.

Even though he wasn't doing it then, he had done it. And it weighed on him. It pained him. He couldn't forgive himself. Mara wanted to know details of Raúl's homosexual experiences too. She'd keep asking until she persuaded him. He'd tell her and Mara would be satisfied. Then she'd tell me. Together we took a perverse delight in what Raúl had done. We said that, deep down, Pablo must be homosexual too.

Raúl arrived in Punta del Este. I told him I'd gone out dancing with a bunch of people I knew the night before.

He didn't care. We both knew I was faithful to him. Raúl told me that Gerardo had got back just as he was about to leave Buenos Aires. That he'd spent Christmas Eve with his family and Mara with hers in the country. Raúl arranged with Mara that she'd pick up the stash from Gerardo's place and leave it at her place. His folks' chauffeur would pick it up from there and, as soon as he found someone to bring it, he'd send it to Punta del Este.

XI

The day after Raúl got there we went to the beach together. I ran into the guy I'd been dancing with the other night. I saw the look of surprise on his face at this chubby guy who was my boyfriend. We barely said hello.

I was staying at Mom's apartment for a few days and then I'd move to Raúl's house. The Pérsicos had a mansion with tons of maids. They called Raúl and me "señorito" and "señorita."

The day Raúl had his last exam in December I went to meet him outside the school. I ran into an ex of his, a guy called Gerónimo. Raúl had told me quite a lot about him. The year before they'd been arrested while buying some psychotropic drugs with a forged prescription. They'd gone to court. Raúl was still on probation and couldn't get a passport. I knew who Gerónimo was as soon as I saw him, even though no one introduced us. I was shocked. I also felt a certain complicity with him and would even have said he was good looking. At that moment Raúl's past didn't bother me.

Still, I was almost always finding some excuse to attack Raúl. I'd make him feel subhuman. Later I'd feel really bad. I'd try to soothe him. But it was hard, I'd already hurt his feelings. I knew all his weaknesses and provoked him. I was always trying to get him mad at me. I wouldn't stop aggravating him until I'd succeeded. Because, in reality, I didn't want to be with him. But I found it impossible to break up with him. I hated Raúl but I couldn't not be with him. And I hated myself: I knew deep down that it was an addiction, just as pernicious as any other. I could stop smoking marijuana if I felt like it. Raúl would do it for me. He was a homo. He was everything bad. I, on the other hand, was good. I did well at school. I didn't fail any subjects. I didn't get busted. I didn't shoot up. What more could they want? I was a shining example of good behavior. Though I did smoke marijuana every day, no one noticed. I was very discreet. Everyone noticed everything Raúl did and if something happened to slip by, he'd make sure he told everybody.

On New Year's Eve I went out for dinner with Mom to some friends' house. Raúl had dinner with his family. Holidays depressed me. I really missed Dad, Susana and her kids. They were celebrating in New York. On Christ-mas Eve and New Year's Eve I felt more like an orphan than ever. It broke my heart. I hated my whole family: those who were with me, those who had left and those who'd died. I was envious of Raúl. Terribly jealous. I felt like murdering his whole family. His parents lived together. He had grandparents, aunts, uncles and cousins. He had all that I'd lost, all that I'd never have again.

Ever since I was fourteen, when I decided to stay in Buenos Aires, I knew that from then on Christmas would be worse than a funeral. That date enraged me, as did Father's Day; I endured them. I suffered like crazy but I didn't tell anyone. On those occasions I wanted to feel alone. I wanted to have a bad time. I had absolutely no intention of changing my ways. The suffering was mine. I clung to it as tightly as I could.

After midnight I met Raúl downtown. I felt more hatred than ever. We went dancing with a bunch of people. While we were in the night club, I started talking to Raúl about Gerónimo. I wanted to know details of their sexual relations. Although I was aware my intentions were evil, something impelled me to ask. I asked him if he'd sucked Gerónimo's cock. He didn't want to answer me. I thought he was right. He shouldn't answer me. I shouldn't ask him that. It was none of my business. But I kept asking. "You're a jerk if you don't answer me. I already know you fucked him. What does it matter if I know the details?" He said he had. I hated him more than ever. I thought he was trash. Why did he answer me? Why did he let me ruin his New Year's Eve like that? He should have told me to fuck off. But he'd answered. He was an idiot. Once again he'd let himself be manipulated.

He'd let me jerk him around. Watching him suffer for what I'd made him remember, I realized I controlled him, and that he was never going to leave me. It calmed me down. I knew I couldn't be without him.

My life revolved around Raúl. I couldn't concentrate on anything else. I spent my life waiting for Raúl to phone me. I didn't hang around with anyone else, except for my two lifelong friends, Mara and Laura. I wasn't interested in school either, though I did well, or any other activity.

On January first, Mom went back to Buenos Aires and I moved to Raúl's house. Raúl's parents wouldn't let us sleep in the same room. I laughed inside because the year before Raúl had invited Gerónimo and they'd slept together. Raúl's mother hated me. She was dying of jealousy. I was Raúl's first girlfriend. She couldn't bear the fact that I was thirty years younger and much thinner than her. I couldn't stand her either. I knew Raúl was actually in love with her.

The last days we spent together were pretty bearable. Raúl and I said goodbye in the bus terminal. We were sad. Raúl waited beside the bus until it left. Later he told me that when he got back home he burst into tears.

Before I left for Europe, I spoke to Raúl on the phone. He told me he really missed me. I felt sorry for him. I was going travelling and he had to stay in Punta del Este by himself all summer.

First I was meeting Luis in Rome. The rest of the trip was unplanned. At some point I would visit my aunt Elena and uncle Guille in Switzerland. A couple of days before I left, Luis called. He said he was in southern Italy and, just in case he couldn't make it back to Rome before I arrived, I should phone him at the house where he was staying. I took down the number and thought nothing of it until I was sitting beside a couple of Italians on the plane. I didn't understand a single word they said. I panicked at the possibility of Luis not being at the airport. Alone in a strange country without knowing the language? I didn't breathe easily until I caught sight of Luis after I passed through customs.

We stayed in the apartment of some friend of Luis's. It was a small room with a double bed. It was so cold. There was no shower.

Luis had been in Italy for several months. He had an Italian girlfriend. He spoke the language perfectly. I affected ignorance of everything, even myself, and sat back and let Luis do everything. Luis didn't have much money left and I was only splitting expenses with him. In order to stretch our cash, we bought cheese, ham and bread that we toasted on the electric heater. When I didn't do things the way Luis liked, he told me I was spoiled and didn't know how to travel.

I disappeared into the stores for several days. Buying clothes calmed me down. But Luis didn't understand that. He dragged me to the Vatican and to as many cathedrals as there were. He also took me to the ruins; according to him they were important, but to me they didn't look like anything other than wasteland. We didn't stop walking all day. We even went out in the rain. Luis wanted me to see every little nook in Rome in one week.

One morning we got caught in a torrential downpour. My shoes got soaked. That night I was burning up. I begged Luis for a day off. Luis didn't understand, he said we had to see Rome. I wanted to go some place with a shower and proper heating. I wanted to be taken care of. Tourism held no appeal for me at all. Luis didn't listen to me. He had a plan and he set it out for me: go to Florence for one day, catch a night train to Paris, spend a day in Paris and then take another night train to Switzerland. "You're crazy, no way I'm doing that." I needed to stay at least one night in a place with a bathtub. We agreed to spend a few days in Florence. During the trip from Rome to Florence I felt only my exhaustion and fever.

When we arrived, we checked into an excellent old hotel in Florence. It struck me as odd to have travelled with my brother and slept in the same bed. One day I asked him something about my legs. He answered that he didn't look at my legs because I was his sister.

As soon as we got settled in the hotel room, I took a bath. Few times in my life had I enjoyed anything more. I took some cold tablets and got into bed. That night we phoned Dad. We asked him if he could send us some money so we could stay in that hotel and take a flight to Zurich. We explained that I was sick and couldn't travel by train. Dad said yes, no problem. I actually had money. Mom had given me some. But only part of it was mine, the rest was for buying her some clothes. I didn't want to tell Dad. I was scared that if I did, he wouldn't give me a cent.

The next morning Luis went out early to walk around. I stayed in bed. I didn't want to see any more palaces or cathedrals or any of that. I told him I wasn't feeling well. I was afraid of offending him if I said no. But at the same time, I felt obliged to go out with him. Luis left and I went out shopping for clothes. I didn't want to buy anything for Mom. But then, I was scared to spend her money. It bugged me that Mom always got me to buy her tons of stuff when I went away. She always managed to annoy me, one way or the other. But for me, buying her clothes was a way of assuaging my guilt for going to see Dad. This time there was more guilt than usual: I was also visiting my aunt Elena. She and Mommy hadn't spoken to each other since the fight over the inheritance four years earlier.

We hadn't been able to get through to my aunt Elena on the phone from Italy. Luis had the wrong number. My aunt and uncle had no idea we were on our way to visit them. As soon as we arrived in Zurich, we got a telephone directory and looked up Estévez.

Uncle Guille came to pick us up at the airport. It was so great to see him! How exciting to be reunited with Elena! It was just wonderful to arrive at the house of people I loved so much. I couldn't believe it. Elena noticed I had a bad cold. She said she'd try to cure me while I was in Switzerland. She made us a meal. I was happy.

Luis insisted we go out and wander around Zurich. I told him I had no interest in Zurich. Luis got mad. "How can you not be interested in getting to know any city?!" I didn't know how to answer him. I told him I'd only come to Zurich to visit my aunt and uncle. Luis wouldn't accept that. Finally we went walking around Zurich. We went to meet Elena at the university. His face lit up when he saw her. "Look at Elena, she looks the same age as her classmates."

I really liked my little cousin. He was four. He went to kindergarten mornings and afternoons. He was obsessed with tits. He was always asking me: "Can I touch your boobs?" I'd laugh and feel embarrassed.

I felt protected in Elena and Guille's house. Everything was comfortable. Sometimes I went to Geneva by myself. I wandered around without anyone telling me where I should go. I'd forgotten all about Raúl, Mara and Pablo. In Switzerland I was fine and didn't need them. Raúl wrote me a letter. I was glad to get it. I knew I'd need him again when I got back to Buenos Aires.

Elena didn't consider it a sin to buy clothes. Moreover, she went shopping with me and advised me. I felt pretty.

Elena and I went to Paris for a week. After Luis had gone back to New York, Elena enthusiastically suggested we go to Paris together. I was thrilled and she thought I was crazy about seeing new places. My joy was from being with Elena, just the two of us, it didn't matter where. For the first time on a trip, there was no obligation to visit museums. I don't know if it was because I was with Elena, but I started to like Paris. Every once in a while I remembered I had to go back to New York soon. Dad's house made me anxious. Going there again seemed like a nightmare. I was fine in Europe. I didn't want to go back to New York. I was going to have to hide again. I couldn't show Dad the clothes I'd bought.

I talked to Elena about my relationship with Dad and my hatred for Susana. Elena was very understanding. She and Dad had gotten along really well when Mom and Dad were married. Later, though they didn't see much of each other, they stayed very fond of each other. Dad had helped her and Guille to make contacts in Switzerland. Elena knew Susana treated us very badly and felt sorry for us.

Full of rage, I boarded an airplane in Zurich for New York. Dad and Luis picked me up from the airport. As soon as I got in the car I swore I'd take revenge on Dad for not letting me invite Raúl to his house. I wasn't really mad about that but it was my excuse to get my revenge for so many other things festering in my guts.

As soon as we got there, Luis told me Dad's house had gone from bad to worse. Pablo appeared, we hugged. We were happy to see each other. "I've got something to tell you," he said. The 24th of December Mara and Raúl had fooled around on us. Although I feigned outrage, it didn't strike me as any big deal. Pablo was much angrier than I was. The first thing that occurred to us was to do the same to them. But we couldn't. Much less then: we were living in the same house. We ran to phone Raúl. He was in Punta del Este. I felt like giving him a piece of my mind. Although Mara pissed me off way more. I knew it had been Mara who'd started it.

Dad got really angry about the phone call to Punta del Este. He burst into my room shouting, beside himself. He said the call was going to cost a fortune and, furthermore, I'd done it without his permission.

Pablo and I went to see Mara. She and her family were staying in a hotel in Manhattan. It was great to see her. "You're so thin," she said. Her parents said I was looking very pretty. When I was alone with Mara I told her I knew what she and Raúl had done. "You're an asshole, a shit, the only thing you care about is fucking everyone else around." She said she was sorry while I was talking. She begged me to forgive her. She swore she'd never do anything like that again. I kept insulting her. "I'm going," I said. Mara burst into tears. That made me want to insult her more. She shouted that I was right, that she'd behaved terribly and she was really sorry. But I didn't believe her. I knew she'd do it again in a minute. I went to the door. Pablo said if I was leaving, so was he. He shot me a look of complicity. He suggested again that he and I should do what they'd done. I was scared. I'd rather stay with Mara. She hugged me and kept crying.

Pablo and Mara told me they were hardly smoking anything. I told them I hadn't smoked at all in Europe. We thought we might as well buy some pot. Pablo thought the stuff they sold in the square was really bad. I suggested we go to my old school. I was sure we could find someone there who could sell us a few joints. Andrés and José were still going to that school and we ran into Andrés that day.

That night I decided to ask Dad for a "salary" increase. Since I'd resolved to stay in Buenos Aires, Dad had been sending me a pittance each month. It didn't even cover my bus fare. But if I wanted to travel, as long as I went by way of New York, Dad would buy me tickets to anywhere in the world. Every time I visited Dad, Mom recommended I ask him to raise my monthly allowance. I had to struggle until I managed it. Adding this matter to my visits with Dad ruined them. I started by telling him the allowance he sent each month wasn't enough. He'd ask me for a list of expenses. "You're crazy! How can you spend so much money?" I'd get furious. I thought about how Dad maintained Susana's kids. What was that? Why did I have to share my dad with them? To top it off, they still had their own dad.

I had endless complaints. I felt awful. It was horrible having to beg Dad for what was rightfully mine. Once again I felt the same anger as on the first Sunday we went out with Susana and her kids. From that day I knew things had changed. That Dad wasn't the same anymore. That I was going to have to share his affection with a whole lot of bloodsuckers. Dad married

Susana when I was eight. I had a premonition that I was losing him forever. Every time I pleaded for an increase I felt like I wasn't his daughter, that I'd become an "outsider," someone meddling in a household she didn't belong to. I wasn't part of my Dad's family. Neither was Luis. Dad had never defended us. I tried to give Dad convincing reasons for the increase. But I panicked when I had to talk to him about money. Dad hated talking about money and so did I.

Just when we were coming to an agreement about my allowance Dad went to his room because Susana was calling him. He came back furious. He asked me to come to his room. Susana was there. Dad and Susana accused Pablo and me of having gone to the school to buy marijuana. Inés had found out from Andrés and told them. "You stupid brats, idiots, you never change, you idiots! And you, Luz, you want me to give you more money. All I'm going to give you is a kick in the ass!" I wasn't scared, I was outraged. I didn't know what to say. Once again I was the lowest of the low. I wanted to leave Dad's house as soon as possible, and never come back. "She's a fucking snitch! She's always sucking up to you! Besides, she smoked too. Her boyfriend used to ask Pablo for joints."

I hadn't been in New York for a week and already I wanted to be back in Buenos Aires. There was no torture worse than being in Dad's house. I wanted to move my flight forward. In spite of everything Dad felt bad. It was obvious that it hurt him that I wanted to leave so soon. And that made me even sadder. Despite all our problems, I adored Dad. But I felt so much bitterness I couldn't tell him about.

The only thing I enjoyed about my stays in New York were my lunches with Dad. Dad was a full professor at NYU. He taught there and was the Deputy Director of the Department of Economic Research. The Director, he told me, had been awarded the Nobel Prize for Economics. Every day at noon I went to the university to meet Dad. We'd go out for lunch in the Village, just the two of us. Sometimes Dad was busy and I'd have to wait for him in his office. I didn't mind. I felt good there. His colleagues and secretary were really nice to me. As far as they were concerned, I was my father's daughter.

The Economics team was investigating the impact on the North American economy of not increasing the annual arms production. Dad explained that the problem was not to investigate what would happen if they decreased arms production but if it remained at current levels. Like most of Dad's work, this proved pretty incomprehensible to me. But Dad seemed very enthusiastic.

"Why teach Economics when you're an astronomer? How do they let you teach classes in Economics when you don't have a degree in it?" I asked.

"I'm pretty much self-educated in Economics but studying Physics has given me the basis to understand any subject."

Dad always let me choose the restaurant. When we were alone together, Dad acted differently. He allowed me things that the mere presence of Susana would have precluded. Sometimes he asked me not to tell anyone what restaurant we'd gone to for lunch. I felt like his accomplice. Chatting with him, I realized he was quite lonely.

Susana was taking painting classes at the New York Studio of Art. It was in the Village too. Dad dropped her off every morning and went to pick her up after work. Susana wouldn't let any of us visit her school. She never took Pablo out for lunch. Mara thought Susana treated Pablo really badly and acted as if she were another one of Dad's kids. In the evening, Dad and I went to pick her up at the Art Studio. When she got into the car she'd look at me with disgust. She started talking about herself and didn't stop until we got home to Bronxville.

Sometimes Pablo and I stayed to have dinner with Mara in the hotel. I waited in the living room until they finished fucking. Then we took the train home. Mara might be Pablo's girlfriend but the one who left with him every night was me. When we got home we'd watch TV in the basement. Or we'd listen to music in the living room. We always hung out together until two or three in the morning.

One night, I had a really sharp pain in my back. Pablo told me he gave really good massages. We were alone in the living room. I accepted his offer of a massage. I was scared, really scared. I lay down on the floor and Pablo massaged my back for a long time. I was sure he was going to kiss me. But he didn't. He didn't dare. We looked at each other not knowing what to say.

Mara and I went out on our own. We went shopping for clothes for her. Later we spent several hours in a café. We talked nonstop. Pablo didn't like going to bars to chat.

One night Pablo and I went out with Mara's family. We went to see a Broadway musical. Dad never took us to see those shows. Ever since I was little, I'd always liked being with Mara's family more than mine. I didn't feel pressured. I felt like I was more likely to be related to Mara's parents than to Daddy and Susana.

Mara's aunt and uncle lived in Bronxville. Mara and her parents were staying there for the last few days they were in New York. Mara told me one of her sisters was having a fling with her cousin. I wasn't surprised. I was jealous: she could fool around with her cousin; me on the other hand, I didn't dare do anything with Pablo and we weren't even blood relations.

Mara, Pablo and Sofía (Mara's mom) and I went to the theater one night in the Village. Pablo and I had already seen the play. Susana had taken us. It was a feminist play. Susana was really into feminism. It was her new hobby since she'd moved to New York. When we came out of the theater, we went to catch the subway out to the train station. It was just the four of us in the subway station. Suddenly a gang of kids on skateboards came up. None of them looked to be over fifteen. They opened their knives. Sofía went pale. I couldn't take my eyes off them. I'd never seen kids like that. They looked old. They played with their knives, threatening and pretending to stab each other. They didn't even look at us. They went down the steps the same way as they'd come up: like a tornado. "There's nothing to be frightened of, they're just kids," said Pablo. "Doesn't matter how young they are, with those knives, they'd chop you to pieces," said Sofía laughing. I wasn't scared. I didn't feel any fear; on the contrary, I was fascinated.

The day Mara left New York, she and Pablo and I smoked some marijuana at home. The weed turned out to be really strong. Pablo and Mara went to Pablo's room. I had an attack of the munchies: I opened the fridge and ate everything in sight. Later on, the three of us smoked at Mara's uncle's house. The Sigals were going to Punta del Este. Raúl was still there. I made Mara swear she wouldn't see him. We said goodbye to Mara later. Pablo and I walked home. "Oh, thank God Mara's gone! I couldn't stand having her around anymore!" Pablo said, once we were outside. It took me completely by surprise. Only much later did I find out that, at home that afternoon, Pablo hadn't been able to get it up.

Despite Dad's opposition, I managed to get my flight to Buenos Aires moved forward. Pablo gave me two of those joints that we'd smoked with Mara to give to Raúl. I said goodbye to Dad as always: with a mixture of hatred and love, and without being able to share with him any of what was really going on with me. I would have liked him to have objected more decisively to my leaving, for him to have told me more clearly what he felt for me. But no, nothing. Once again I was going back to the old routine: Mom, Ester, Raúl.

XII

Mommy and Raúl came to pick me up from the airport. It was such a relief to see them! Raúl was studying for his March exams. Mom announced that she had various matters to discuss with me. She was determined that she and I would be going to Punta del Este the following day. I noticed she was on the warpath. "And this time you won't be getting your own way," she assured me. I, however, was sure I'd get my own way: I would be staying in Buenos Aires with Raúl.

As soon as we got home, Mom started in on the interrogation. What was this about some grass we'd bought from a certain Gerardo? "I didn't buy any grass off any Gerardo," I answered. Mom took out a letter: it was from Mara. It had arrived after I'd left for Europe. In the letter, she wrote about Gerardo, Christmas Eve, the impossibility of getting the grass to Raúl's family's chauffeur and her final decision to leave it hidden inside her guitar.

Mom was angry with me, but not too much. I insisted I had nothing to do with the pot and that, anyway, I didn't smoke up anymore. I thought—I told her—that drugs made people stupid. "If Raúl's your boyfriend and Mara your best friend, then one way or another you must have had something to do with it," said Mom.

Mom told me that, as well as writing me a letter, Mara had written a very similar one to Pablo, from Colorado. She accidentally left the letter to Pablo in a rental car. They found it under a seat and sent it to Mara's father. When they were back in Punta del Este, Mara stole fifty dollars from her mother. Her parents noticed, then it all came out. Although they'd never hit their kids, that time Mara's father practically killed her. She said that he himself had taken the grass out of the bottom of the guitar and flushed it down the toilet.

Mara's father went to talk to Raúl's parents. The maid answered. Raúl's father apologized for not having time but he had to do the grocery shopping. Mara's insisted: he couldn't believe they didn't want to listen to him. Finally, Raúl's mother received him, but without much interest.

I was embarrassed to be involved in this business. I was worried about losing my freedom. "You're going to have to drag me if you think I'm going to Punta del Este with you," I screamed. Mom was persuaded I wasn't going. During the time Mom was away, I had to stay at my grandmother's place.

I said goodbye to Mom and went over to Raúl's. We smoked the joints I'd brought from New York. "Watch it, this dope is really weird," I warned him. He gave me a "and who are you to tell me anything about dope" look. Before we smoked up, we were about to fuck. But we didn't. After we smoked, we again thought about fucking.

Then I noticed that Raúl couldn't get it up. "No, I don't know what's wrong with me, but I can't," said Raúl. "I've spent the last two months waiting for you to get back and now I can't get it up," he added. He was feeling worse and worse and I didn't know what to do. I started crying. I didn't understand what was going on. Just a little while before, he'd been hard. I told him it didn't matter, not to worry. But later I said maybe he'd become impotent. "If you say things like that, I'll never get it up." I felt bad. He was right.

We couldn't take the effects of that pot anymore, so we went downstairs to the kitchen to drink some milk. It didn't help at all. After a few hours, we started to get back to normal. We felt a lot better. We finally fucked. I forgot to put in my diaphragm.

Everything was strange at my grandmother's place. Mara came over one morning. We talked about the hassle over the dope. Meanwhile my grandmother did nothing but shout orders at me. Mara was disturbed by the way she treated me. She thought it must be worse than being in the army.

On Friday, Raúl told me over the phone that he'd bought me a Siamese cat. He had it at his house. That night, according to Clara, I had to go out for dinner to one of her nieces' place. We got back early. I mentioned to Clara that I was going over to Raúl's. She said no. I couldn't believe my ears. What do you mean no? Who was she to tell me no? Never in my life had I not been allowed out on a Friday night. I always went where I wanted and until whatever time. "Raúl's house is nearby, I'm only going for a while then I'll be back, I want to see the Siamese cat he bought me!" She said no again. I asked why not. "I'm frightened for you to go out alone. It's late. Go to bed and stop making such a fuss." Nothing like that had ever happened to me before. There was no way of convincing her. I had to phone Raúl and tell him I couldn't come over to his house because my grandmother wouldn't let me.

The next day I met the cat. It looked like the one I'd had when I was little. Ester thought Siamese cats were very well-mannered. When I was five, we adopted two stray cats. Luis and I dressed them in dolls' clothes. The cats were infested with fleas and we were covered in bites. Ester hated those cats. They peed and pooped all over the house. One day, Ester asked Mom to choose between her or the cats. Mom opted for Ester. But luckily, Ester got really attached to my Siamese cat.

Raúl and I took the cat to the vet's. Since it was on the way, we went to my grandmother's place. Clara, anxious and indisposed, asked me several times if the cat had fleas. I told her it didn't. How could he? The night before, Raúl had practically drowned him in flea powder! Even so, it was useless: Clara made a scene. She shouted at us to get the cat out of there and obliged me to shut it in my room.

That night, as usual, we hung out at Raúl's. Near dawn, a friend rang the doorbell. He'd brought some quaaludes. I'd never taken them before but I'd heard the name tons of times.

The year before, Laura and I had even bought some quaaludes with one of her uncle's prescription slips we'd filled in. But we never got up the nerve to take them. That night I took a 'lude and a half.

I had heard that quaaludes were aphrodisiacs. Raúl thought if someone took a 'lude they'd fuck anyone.

The quaaludes had a really strange effect on me. I'd never felt anything like it. I wanted Raúl's friends to leave. I wanted to fuck him. I forgot to put in my diaphragm again. I called my grandmother. She was worried about me. It was six in-the morning. She shouted that I should come home that instant.

We hadn't seen Mara for three weeks. Her parents had forbidden her to get in touch with me. At first, I was relieved, I couldn't stand being with her all the time any-more, but at the same time it seemed unfair. Once again I was the marginal one. According to Mara's father, Raúl was a murderer, a hardened drug addict, the worst thing that could ever have happened in his daughter's life was to have met Raúl.

Mara's father had told Pablo that if he happened to see Raúl walking down the street, he wouldn't hesitate to run him over with his car.

Mara wasn't allowed to see me, even though I hadn't been involved in the dope deal. They said it wasn't because of me but my relationship with Raúl and Pablo.

I was jealous that Mara's parents cared so much about her. I was sure that mine would never have had the firmness to for-bid me from seeing someone. I would have liked them to forbid me from seeing everyone. Much as Mara complained that they wouldn't let her see anyone and kept her locked up at home all day, she felt very important. And me, less important than ever. I had become the illegal friend. I wasn't allowed to go to Mara's family's place in the country for weekends anymore.

No matter how much of a fuss Mara kicked up, they wouldn't let her go anywhere. She had to stay home Saturdays and Sundays without seeing anyone. Mara's father had always been easy to convince, but this time he wouldn't budge. He was unshakable. I was shocked. I thought he'd forget about her being grounded. But no, he stood fast.

One Saturday afternoon we were at Raúl's and Mara phoned. I thought she'd just called to say hello and find out what we were up to. But no. She was all excited. She told Raúl to get me to come to the phone as well: "You guys, guess what I found?" "What?" "The grass. Yeah, I found the grass; I didn't know what to do with myself anymore, being grounded for so long, so I started looking through my folks' clothes. Behind a pile of my dad's shirts I found the grass. And, know what? Half of it's gone."

XIII

Mom came back from Punta del Este. The cat and I settled in back home. I was glad that Mom and Ester welcomed the cat so enthusiastically. School would start soon. I was going into fourth year. Raúl into fifth. I didn't know what school to go to. I was sure I wanted to change schools. I couldn't stand staying in the same one as Raúl.

The rest of the schools all seemed the same to me. I thought they were just as bad as each other. I'd been to a different school for each year of high school: I went through the first half of first year at Liceo 5, until I moved to New York; second year at Melville High School, where they called it "ninth grade." For third year, back in Buenos Aires, I refused to go back to Liceo 5. I wanted to go to a coed school, without a uniform and not very demanding. In Buenos Aires, there were only two schools that didn't require uniforms; I chose one, the Instituto Roosevelt.

The Instituto Roosevelt turned out to be a hodgepodge of drug addicts who'd been kicked out of other schools and had serious learning difficulties. My classmates didn't study anything ever. My teachers asked me what I was doing there. They thought I was too intelligent. At recess, some of the kids got together to smoke marijuana in the courtyard. Others bought Coca Cola and added whiskey they'd brought from home. I was a very good student. But I missed a lot of classes, I never managed to go for a full week.

One day, some kids from fourth year leaned into my classroom. They told me it was a Jewish holiday and I should ask if I could leave. The prefect gave me permission. The next day I found out that it hadn't been a Jewish holiday. The prefect wanted to mark me absent. I told her it wasn't fair, that anyone could have made that mistake.

One morning, Pablo was arriving home from a trip. While we were at school Raúl decided we should ask for permission to go and welcome him home. Claudia, a friend of ours, was going to come too. The principal agreed. We left school halfway through the morning. We called Pablo from a pay phone on Cabildo Avenue and were told he hadn't arrived yet. "The fact is, it's ridiculous that the principal should let us leave school at 11 o'clock in the morning to go see Pablo when we've got the whole afternoon free," said Raúl.

As we walked along Cabildo towards the café we usually went to after school, we saw tons of cops. Raúl guessed they were conducting some operation. We went into the café. I went to the bathroom. When I came out, I saw that Claudia and Raúl were surrounded by cops. They asked to see my ID. I handed them the ID card I'd had since I was a baby. Raúl had his ID in order and Claudia didn't have any on her.

They told Claudia to go and Raúl and me to come with them. They were taking us to the station to ask us some questions. In the wagon they told me they were taking me in because my ID wasn't up-to-date and Raúl as an associate. They asked us if we were skipping. We said no. But we couldn't tell them the principal had let us leave before the bell, they'd close down the school.

At the police station they asked us what we were doing, where we lived, what our parents did for a living and why we were walking the streets at that hour of the morning. They ordered us to call home and get someone to come and get us. Before letting us leave, they made us sign a statement that we'd skipped school. Later I realized the real reason they'd taken me in was because they considered my behavior suspicious: I'd gone into the bathroom when they came into the café.

My third year was ending and I could barely stand that school anymore. In literature class one day we were told we'd have to read *El Cid*. One guy, as he wrote down the name of the poem, asked who'd written it. They answered that it was anonymous. He asked what that meant. "That nobody wrote it, you moron!" answered another kid.

Mom and I went to check out a private school that was two blocks away from home. They had a place for me in the fourth year but Mom thought it was really expensive. "I can't afford it, ask your dad to raise your allowance." When I talked to Dad on the phone he objected. "Get by on what you have. You don't need to go to a private school." I got really angry. "You always paid for Susana's kids to go to private schools!" He asked me how much I'd need and promised to send it as soon as possible.

A month after starting at the new school, I felt faint at recess one day. I tried to cover it up, not to say anything to anyone. I'd just started there, I didn't want to draw attention to myself, but when I went up to the classroom, the teacher said I looked pale. She asked me what was wrong. She suggested I call home and get someone to come and pick me up.

My period was late. I decided to tell Mom. I thought it would be better for Mom to know straightaway in case I was pregnant. Mom suggested I make an appointment with the gynecologist. The doctor didn't think I was pregnant. She prescribed some pills to bring on my period. I told Mara that maybe I was pregnant. "If you are pregnant, you hide it very well, because you don't look an ounce heavier." I thought she was very observant.

I started getting worried: in the leaflet that came with the pills, it said that menstruation would take, at most, ten days to come on. And those ten days had now passed. Mom spoke to the gynecologist. She told us not to worry. Mom calmed down and tried to calm me down. But I knew things weren't as the gynecologist said. I told Raúl. On the one hand, I thought it would be better not to be pregnant, but on the other, I wanted to be. I imagined Raúl would be nice to me, would make me feel special. Raúl wanted me to be pregnant.

The first times I fucked Raúl, we used rubbers that were in the desk in my room. That room used to be my brother's. The box of condoms had been left there. I didn't know what was in that box. Before we started going out, Raúl saw the rubbers in my desk by chance. He assumed I'd already done it. He asked Pablo if I were a virgin. Pablo said probably not. So Raúl had no doubts that I had fucked someone before. But when he asked me, I told him I was still a virgin. He couldn't believe I didn't know there were rubbers in my room. I told him that they were my brother's and I had nothing to do with it. It had never occurred to me to open the box or to throw it out. Raúl was embarrassed to buy rubbers. I thought that was outrageous: he was the man and it was up to him to buy them.

A while later I decided the logical thing would be for me to get a diaphragm. I went to see the gynecologist. She asked me how old I was, if I had a boyfriend and not much else. I didn't understand anything. I was afraid the gynecologist might ask me questions I didn't know the answers to. She also talked about the correct use of contraceptives and the danger of pregnancy. I thought she was a drag and that she'd never get around to writing me out a prescription and letting me out of the examining room.

I ate at Laura's that evening. I told her I'd got a prescription for a diaphragm and I wanted to buy it, but I didn't have any money. Mom never had any cash. If I expected her to give me money I'd never have any. I didn't want to ask Raúl either. Laura said she'd buy it for me. We decided to go right then. Laura thought an evening excursion to buy a diaphragm would be really fun. The pharmacy was open late and it was almost dark when they handed me the package through a little window. We opened it at Laura's house. It contained a diaphragm, a tube of vaginal cream and something for inserting it. When I saw the diaphragm I realized it was the same thing Mara had shown me when we were twelve. She'd told me it was a condom and we wondered how they used it. I knew it wasn't a rubber now but I still had no idea where or how to put it in.

Not even a year had gone by and I was in the gynecologist's office for the third time. Alone. Almost sure I was pregnant. I told the doctor that ten days had passed since I took the pills and nothing had changed. She wanted to examine me. With a gloved hand she felt me inside. "Yes, your uterus is noticeably enlarged... you're pregnant." I didn't know what I was feeling. I was confused. I couldn't imagine myself with a baby. It all seemed like a game. At that moment there was no doubt I'd have an abortion and it didn't really bother me. I chose to look at it as a formality. The doctor called Mom. She told her I was pregnant. Mom came to the office so the three of us could discuss it. Actually, the two of them talked, I had nothing to say.

When I got home I called Raúl. I told him I was pregnant. He was glad of this proof of his fertility. He came over for dinner. Mom asked him if he was up on the news. Raúl answered yes, enthusiastically. Mom didn't hide her shock. We saw an advantage: until the abortion, we didn't have to be careful. The truth was that Raúl was proud of himself and I was glad to know I could have kids. I'd always wondered about that. Now that I had to have an abortion, I thought I was at the ideal age. Obviously I wasn't going to have a baby at sixteen. On the other hand, I imagined having an abortion when you're older must be awfully sad. You'd feel like a murderer.

Nevertheless, more than once I counted the months left until my baby would supposedly be born. At those times, I didn't want Raúl to be the father. I had a terrible feeling if I had an abortion, I'd regret it enormously and become an old maid. One day, after fucking Raúl, I told him I felt bad about having an abortion, that I didn't want to. He was really sweet to me.

Mom took care of finding an abortionist. I told her I could look after it just as well. I had several friends who'd had abortions. But Mom asked me to leave it in her hands. She told me I was a brat who didn't think about anything I did and that's why things like getting pregnant happened to me. I answered that if she wanted to help me then fine, but not to mock me and I could just as well make my own arrangements without any help from her.

Raúl decided to tell his dad. His dad offered to pay for the abortion. But he also told us not to be afraid to do what we wanted. If we wanted to get married and have the baby, he didn't see anything wrong with that. He left it entirely up to us.

Mara, Pablo, Laura and Claudia knew. But I didn't want anyone else to find out. I didn't know what to think about my situation. My opinions were very changeable. I didn't really think about it all that much. I kept going to school and seeing my friends.

Before school started, Raúl had asked me if I wanted to drop acid. I'd never done acid before. I didn't have anything against it either, especially since I wasn't going to be taking it every day. Raúl showed me some strips of paper with little pictures of cartoon characters on them. Each one was a tab of acid. He took one, I took a half. He told me to suck on the paper until it dissolved in my mouth. While I was taking the acid, I went to have a shower. Mom came in the bathroom. I was scared I was going to swallow the tab. Mom asked me what we were doing that night. I answered that we were going out for dinner. I didn't know what to wear. Nothing seemed to fit right, I was too skinny. It was the first time in my life I thought I was skinny.

We went to eat at the Rodeo in Recoleta. It was three blocks from home. While we were in the restaurant, the acid started to kick in. Seeing the word "sauerkraut" on the menu sent me off on a giggle fit and the old ladies at the next table looked deformed. We met a friend of Raúl's. He noticed right away we were on a weird trip. I felt he was one of us. After dinner we went to see Claudia. She thought that for being on acid we weren't too off our heads.

I'd never even mention drugs to my classmates at the new school. I didn't want to get a bad reputation. But I felt different from them. I thought they were very innocent. I supposed all the girls must be virgins. I told them I had a boyfriend. I felt I'd never be able to be like the other kids at school: they had families. It struck me as unusual that they weren't allowed to miss classes. Dad didn't even know what school I went to and Mom didn't know when. I hated the kids in my class. Skipping seemed like the stupidest thing in the world to me. Why should I bother getting up early and wandering around the streets when I could be sleeping in at home? With the pregnancy on top of it all, I felt there was an abyss between me and my classmates.

Mom told me that Raúl's parents had offered to pay for the abortion. Mom and Raúl's mother had met in a café to discuss it; Mom didn't accept but said she'd think about it. Raúl's mother understood perfectly that given the situation I might not be comfortable going to their house but she invited Raúl and me to see *Apocalypse Now* anyway. I thought it was horrible. I wanted to get out of there as soon as possible.

One doctor didn't want to perform the abortion because I was a minor. Another was going to charge what Mom considered an unreasonable amount of money. Finally, Mom found a suitable doctor. She took me to the appointment. His office was in Barrio Norte. On the door was a plaque that read: "Doctor Esteban Giménez Quiroga." We had to wait a long time in a waiting room full of people. Mostly women with their husbands or women on their own. Mommy and I went in. The doctor told me to undress and lie down on the examining table with my legs apart. He put on some rubber gloves. While he examined me he asked how old I was. "Eighteen." The look on his face said I don't believe you for a second. He asked me what I did. I answered that I'd finished high school the year before and wasn't doing anything. I couldn't think of anything I might be doing. He gave me advice about how it would do me good to study or work, make something of my life. Then he said, sure enough, I was pregnant. We set the date for the abortion: the following Saturday afternoon. In four days time.

Mommy told me Ester suspected what was going on and had asked her. Mom told her that yes, I was pregnant. Ester burst into tears. Mommy explained that for Ester, it was a terrible thing. I felt really sorry for Ester.

I told Raúl the abortion would be that very Saturday. He was surprised it could be so soon. I calculated that I was a month and a half pregnant.

The Friday before the abortion I had diarrhea. Mom thought it must be from fear. But I wasn't scared. Saturday morning I ate several pieces of toast. The abortion would be in the afternoon and the doctor said I wasn't to eat anything after breakfast.

The abortion was to be done in a place outside the city. Mom took me in the car. Raúl came too. We went towards Olivos or Florida, I wasn't really sure. I wasn't nervous at all. We arrived at a quiet, secluded spot. There was no one in the street. On the door was a plaque that read: "Esteban Giménez." In a place like that, it seemed, one surname was enough.

Through the peephole a lady said that only one companion was allowed in. Raúl stayed outside. The house was ugly, dark. The curtains were torn and half falling off. A woman came tottering down the staircase. It was my turn. I said goodbye to Mom. I went up the same stairs alone. I went into the room. The doctor was there. He told me to take off my pants. He asked me how old I'd told him I was. "Eighteen," I lied again.

I was left with the nurse. She ordered me to lie down on the examining table. She asked me to stretch out my arms. She secured them at my sides. Then she tied my legs open. I was shocked. I'd never had an operation. It would be the first time I'd have a general anesthetic. No one told me what it would be like. I was used to friendlier doctors who told me step by step what they were doing. This one didn't say a word to me and had them tie me down as if I were a piece of meat.

The nurse announced she was going to anesthetize me. She squeezed my arm with a really tight elastic and jabbed the needle in. But nothing happened. She tried again. I started to get scared. She said my veins were really hard to find. She tried one more time. She gave up. She called the doctor. Instead of giving me the injection in the arm, he gave it to me in the wrist. Immediately I felt my arm going to sleep and the same current flowing through my whole body like a flash of lightning.

I woke up in a strange bed with the feeling of having something weird in my panties. Mommy was at my side. She asked me if I could get up. I sat up. There was nothing in my panties. I put my pants on feeling completely dizzy and went to where the doctor was. He prescribed an antibiotic. He told me to stay in bed for one day, not to have intercourse for twenty, and that he hoped never to see me again.

The three of us went home in the car without exchanging a single word. I had nothing to say. Raúl didn't open his mouth. When we got home, I went to bed. Raúl went to tell his parents it had all gone okay. Laura phoned. She came over to see me. Claudia and Mara called too. I wanted to be spoiled, but no one did it the way I'd hoped. Raúl came back with some really nice pastries. I was scared that Raúl wouldn't love me after the abortion.

At dawn the next day I had a feeling of deep emptiness. I went to the kitchen and ate tons of pastries, as many as I felt like, without bothering to take the box out of the fridge.

XIV

Mom said, "Luz, wake up, you're in Buenos Aires." It was February, I'd got back from New York the previous day. That time I'd stayed at Luis's place, which Dad accepted without any trouble. I would have liked him to have insisted I stay at his house, but he didn't. He thought it sufficient to promise me we'd go out for dinner and lunch as often as I wanted and, whenever I felt like eating at his house, all I had to do was ask.

The first night I went for dinner at Dad's. I would have given anything for him to have begged me to stay. But no. He came out with me to hail a taxi. I felt like the lowest piece of shit on earth. "Daddy, please, how can you do this to me? How can you be such a bastard?" I thought as we said goodbye.

Luis was living with Ornella, his girlfriend. I got along well with Ornella. I knew I'd get along with any girlfriend of Luis's. Any person Luis chose, I would like as well. Ornella was Italian. They spoke Italian to each other. I didn't understand a single word.

The day after my arrival, Luis told me Dad had sold the place in the country. I wanted to die. How could he not have told me anything!? Dad was the worst.

That night I couldn't sleep. I cried into the pillow. I hated Dad more than ever. I imagined that, from then on, I'd have to stay in Buenos Aires every weekend. Even though I didn't go out to the country place very often, knowing it was there was reassuring. Dad had confined me to the city. I thought I'd go crazy.

At that time, Dad was running a company that was about to propose a development project for a sixty-acre district of New York City. Other companies had already tried but to no avail: the Neighborhood Committee vetoed the proposals. Dad was sure they'd be successful. The company's capital came from a group of Argentinians who'd made a lot of money during the last military dictatorship. They were of Italian descent. Dad said they hadn't even finished high school. They didn't speak a word of English. Dad had become an executive with a chauffeur and not a spare moment to catch his breath. He didn't take vacations. He received constant phone calls wherever he went, even in the dentist's chair.

Dad's colleagues fooled around on their wives and joked with Dad about getting the contract by having an affair with the chairwoman of the Residents Committee.

Dad had never had a job like that. It was the first time I'd seen him in such an elegant office surrounded by such awful people.

Dad and I went out for lunch. I told him Luis had told me about the place in the country. He answered that he hadn't actually wanted to sell it. But when he left Argentina he'd given power of attorney to Susana's mother. She had arranged the sale without consulting them. I couldn't believe such stupidity. Even worse: I couldn't even blame Dad. Susana's mother had power of attorney? Was my dad that much of an idiot? He asked me not to reproach him, Susana had already screamed at him enough. Dad tried to console me. He told me it wasn't actually the place itself I was sorry to lose, just that it was the last thing he had left in Argentina.

While I was in New York, Raúl was on vacation in Búzios in Brazil. At the beginning of February we got together in Punta del Este. A while after the abortion, things with Raúl started going from bad to worse. We fought all the time. I couldn't stand that all he ever did was take drugs. When the relationship got too tense, Raúl would take off. He'd say he never wanted to see me again. He'd hang up on me. I would run over to his house and beg him to keep going out with me. I'd cry. I'd tell him to do what he liked, not to pay any attention to me. I'd promise him anything if he'd stay with me. Raúl would finally agree. But he'd swear if we started arguing again there wouldn't be any more getting back together.

Raúl came to pick me up at the airport. When I got into the car he warned me not ever to make any more remarks about his druggyness; that he was going to do as many drugs as he felt like. I felt lonely, very lonely. I sensed he was going to leave me any time now. I hated my dependence on Raúl, but I couldn't help it. I answered that I didn't want to fuck him around anymore either. I tried to change the subject, tell him something funny. I made an attempt. However, we didn't manage to get along very well. Before a week had gone by, Raúl wanted to go back to Buenos Aires. I didn't.

Raúl suggested we should split up. I was in despair! But at the same time, I realized the situation was hopeless. I'd never fucked another guy and wondered what it would be like, but I couldn't imagine being anyone's girlfriend except Raúl's. I thought there must be something different to fucking than what Raúl and I did. It pissed me off that Raúl wasn't interested in what I felt. He touched me just enough so he could come. I couldn't wait for him to come because I never felt any pleasure. It also pissed me off that he was so disgusted by me when I had my period. And since he was also disgusted by the diaphragm cream, I changed methods of contraception: I went on the pill, even though I knew it wasn't the best.

Carla arrived. Carla was a friend of Raúl's. She'd been Pablo's first girlfriend. At that time she was buying dope off Pablo and Raúl. Carla said I could stay at her place. Her dad had rented a house in Manantiales. Raúl said I should stay at his house even though he was going back to Buenos Aires. I thought that was ridiculous. What if I wanted to go out with another guy? I accepted Carla's offer.

On the one hand, I was drawn to Carla; but on the other, she scared me. During meals at their house, they always talked about bums and hemorrhoids and shitting.

Carla had brought tons of cocaine. We took it morning, noon and night. And so we were constantly sniffling. Carla's dad didn't know what to give us anymore to cure us of those colds. The only thing that gave us momentary relief was to snort more cocaine.

I listened with admiration and horror to Carla's sexual adventures: she'd fucked all the men in a group of actor friends and at the same time was best friends with their girlfriends. They had group sex: she and a friend and her friend's boyfriend, all three of them together. She asked if Raúl, Pablo, Mara and I had ever done that. I said no.

I decided to go back to Buenos Aires to talk to Raúl. I wanted us to get back together. Carla thought it wasn't worth it and encouraged me to stay single. She told me what life was like without a boyfriend. She said I'd have to face up to going to bars on my own. "You're not going to be a one-man woman anymore."

The prospects Carla described horrified me. Mom had no idea I was coming back. No one was home. There was an eggplant quiche in the fridge that Ester had made. When I saw it, I felt like I was home.

I went to Raúl's that night. He was on his own. We acted as if nothing had happened. Pablo phoned after a while. "No, not yet," Raúl said. I imagined Pablo had asked if he'd told me to fuck off. I got mad. But on the other hand, Pablo and Mara weren't going out any-more and it didn't seem possible for Raúl and me to keep seeing each other. We went to Raúl's parents' room and fucked there.

The next morning the maid woke us up. Juan, Raúl's math tutor, had arrived. Juan was doing a Mathematics degree in the Faculty of Sciences of the National University of Buenos Aires. I'd met him a few months earlier, when Raúl was studying for his chemistry exam. I thought he was cute. I said hi when I went downstairs for breakfast. Raúl thought Juan was an excellent teacher.

Mom and I went back to Punta del Este very early the next morning. Mom said it was a lucky thing Carla had invited me to stay at her place because there was no room for me at the house she was going to. I was hurt but I pretended it didn't matter and that I could get along perfectly well without her.

As soon as I got there, I ran into Damián, a guy who'd asked me out a few days before. I told him I'd broken up with my boyfriend and we decided to go out that night. "He's going to fuck you," a friend said to me. "What do I care?" I answered.

Damián invited me over to his house. After a while, we fucked. I was really scared: I was trembling while he took my clothes off. I didn't tell him. I didn't feel any pleasure either, it was repulsive. It seemed horrible that he was touching and kissing me. He said he loved me and I felt even more revulsion: it was a lie. I started to feel really awful. I didn't know what I was doing there. Why was I in bed with that guy? I wanted to leave as soon as possible. He didn't know what was wrong with me. He went with me to get a taxi. I never wanted to see him again.

The next night, Carla and I went downtown. Two guys we knew gave us a lift back to Manantiales. The four of us sat around talking and snorting coke. I liked one of the guys. We went to my room. Though I didn't feel any pleasure, at least I found him attractive. I liked his body. I was proud to have fucked a guy I thought was so good looking. He left first thing in the morning. It had rained and the windows of the room were open. Our clothes were soaked. I lent him a pair of my pants.

Carla's dad was getting divorced from his second wife. A stream of really strange women passed through his house. Platinum blondes that looked like hookers.

One day Mom came over to visit me at Carla's. In passing she asked if her dad were there. I realized she hadn't actually come to see me but to try to pick up Carla's dad. I felt pissed off, and sorry for her.

We met a friend of Carla's. He'd brought some coke from Bolivia. Apparently he was really famous. He sold drugs to several comic actors. Carla went out with him and didn't come back for two days. I didn't know how to act without Carla there.

I realized I didn't matter to Carla, and her dealer friend was all she was interested in. I remembered Carla telling me that more than likely the dealer wasn't even interested in her. Nevertheless, she'd been with him for two days. Mommy, when she found out what was going on, said I could come and sleep on the couch at her house.

I didn't know when school was starting. I didn't mind missing the first few days. I was starting fifth year. I didn't even want to think about finishing high school. A couple of days before going back to Buenos Aires, Carla and I dropped a tab of acid each. We put henna in our hair. I came out half red-head. The night before I left, I met up with the guy whom I'd lent a pair of pants and he gave them back.

As soon as I got back to Buenos Aires, I called Raúl. He came over and we fucked. He thought I was skinny, said my tits were smaller. Mom arrived after Raúl left. She saw me in my underwear and advised me that if I wanted to break up with Raúl, I shouldn't hang around with him in my panties.

Not seeing Raúl every day made me feel completely miserable. I spent all the time hoping he'd phone me. I fucked all his friends without really caring who they were. I felt like a filthy slut. I ate constantly. I was getting fatter all the time. When I woke up, I'd remember I wasn't going out with Raúl anymore and get worried. I wanted to die.

I made friends with a girl at school. Her name was Sonia. She lived in Palermo Chico. Sonia's mother owned villas and a sugar plantation way up north. Her father was a racing car driver, he'd been left paralyzed by an accident during a race. I was fascinated by Sonia's upper crust past. Sonia told me that her mother and her second husband did drugs and sometimes couples who were friends of theirs stayed overnight to sleep with them. Sonia's mother's room took up a whole floor of the house. The kids weren't allowed in it.

I was going to New York for the month of July. I was flying with Pablo. I hated him then. He was always with Raúl. They injected cocaine and were selling it too.

The day I was leaving for New York, Sonia told me her mother had gone away and the door of her room was unlocked. She asked me to help her search it. She wanted to find some drugs so later she could throw it back in her mother's face.

Sonia's mother's room had mirrors on the ceiling. In another room, there was a sauna. Sonia told me her boyfriend had laughed when he saw the mirrors on the ceiling. I couldn't see why. First we went through the bathroom. There were all kinds of half-used tubes of cream. The leaflets were in English. They were creams to facilitate orgasms in women, immediately after childbirth; to make men take longer to come. I couldn't believe my eyes. I'd never have suspected such things existed. Sonia didn't seem too bothered, more like proud. I didn't understand what of. She was obsessed with finding drugs. Sonia asked me if I knew what a vibrator was. I did. I'd seen loads of them in the display windows of the sex shops in the States. Sonia took one out of the bathroom cupboard.

Before leaving for Ezeiza, I was bouncing off the walls at home not knowing what to do. I decided to smoke a cigarette. I went to Mom's desk and got one out. Then another. I smoked several. I reached the conclusion that I hadn't smoked before because I didn't know how, but now I'd learned. I bought a pack.

In the plane Pablo took a sleeping pill and offered me one. I declined. Pablo told me he thought it was really stupid that I was fucking anyone and everyone because I had a really nice body and was going to ruin it. I assured him I wasn't going to fuck just anyone anymore. Pablo told me about shooting cocaine. He said he didn't like it but Raúl did.

When we were in New York, Pablo thought we should drop some acid. We took some and went out dancing. I, like Pablo, thought I had a great body, but I was so fat I couldn't fit into any of my clothes. I loved going out with Pablo. We drank a lot. I liked Pablo, I was more attracted to him than ever. But I couldn't imagine how we'd be able to face each other if we kissed. It couldn't happen. Dad and Susana had forbidden it.

I went to bed as soon as we got home. Pablo knocked on my door. I was sure something was going to happen between us. Both of us, I thought, wanted to make love. More than that: I was convinced we were both dying to. But Pablo didn't dare try anything. And neither did I. When I opened the door he asked me if I wanted to go down to the kitchen with him for some ice cream. Before we went to bed, we kissed on the cheek and each went to our own room.

When I got back from that trip to New York I felt worse than ever. Mornings depressed me. I wanted to see Raúl, but he didn't give a shit about me. Pablo, who was back too, said as soon as he finished his military service, he was going to go live in New York. I didn't believe him.

I started to worry about my future. I didn't know what to do when I finished high school.

I realized I liked literature and math. I didn't know which one to study. One day Claudia showed me a book by Lewis Carroll. She told me he'd been a mathematician and, later, a writer. I was really excited. I felt like I'd found my vocation. I devoted several pages of my diary to my happiness at having discovered my vocation. I thought I'd do a double major in Letters and Mathematics.

Laura was going to major in Physics. She'd been preparing for the entrance exam since the beginning of the year. Going to the University of Buenos Aires terrified me.

Bit by bit I started to see Raúl again. But we weren't a couple like before. We fucked once in a while and that was it.

One day, Carla phoned. She'd been committed to a psychiatric clinic. She asked me to let Raúl know. I was thrilled to be the go-between. I felt important. I went for dinner at Raúl's. I told him about Carla. All of a sudden, Raúl said he didn't want to fuck me anymore. I felt bad. I didn't understand and Raúl didn't give me any explanation.

That year, 1981, Luis graduated with a degree in Engineering. Mom went to visit him. I stayed with Ester. I loved staying with Ester. She still took better care of me than anyone. But on the weekends she went home and I was left on my own.

Raúl had a party for his birthday. He invited me and I felt really proud. The party was a bash. Everyone was off their heads, All of a sudden, all the guests disappeared, I couldn't see why. A neighbor had called the cops. Pablo, Raúl and I were left. Pablo finally left and I went to bed with Raúl.

Two days later, Raúl phoned me. He was whispering. It seemed like he was crying. He said he was in an empty apartment upstairs from his. A guy who he and Pablo sold cocaine to had been busted. "He squealed on me." When the police came looking for him, the doorman asked to see their warrant. Since they didn't have one, he didn't let them in. Raúl burst into tears while he was telling me. The police came back later with a warrant. The cops were still waiting in his house. They promised they wouldn't leave until he came back.

Raúl had already been arrested for forging quaalude prescriptions. The case wasn't closed yet. If he got caught again, he'd be sent directly to Devoto Penitentiary. Raúl called Pablo and told him to make himself scarce from his house because if they ended up arresting him, he'd squeal. Raúl asked me to come and visit him in the apartment where he was hiding.

I didn't say anything to Mom and went over to see Raúl. At dinner time, his mom came up with food. Raúl was hiding in an empty room with just a mattress and a television with the volume down really low. He kept the blinds shut.

That night Raúl said he'd been wanting to get back together with me for a while, for us to be a couple again. I had my doubts but what could I say. We got back together.

The police left Raúl a date and time for a lineup with the kid who'd squealed on him. Whether or not he went to Devoto depended on how it went.

The day of the lineup, Raúl said if he didn't phone me that afternoon, it would mean he'd been sent to Devoto. When I got home from school, I asked Ester if anyone had called. She said no. It scared me. Even though I also thought that if Raúl was sent to Devoto it would be for the best, the only way we could actually break up. I was sure I'd done the wrong thing in getting back with Raúl.

Halfway through the afternoon, Raúl called. It had all gone fine.

Mara told me Pablo had gone to live in New York. He had been thinking of going the following week, but when the police went to pick up Raúl, he decided to move his flight forward. Mara said she'd cried at his farewell party, she laughed and said she cried easily. Me, I didn't even know exactly what day he'd left.

XV

Laura had started a Physics degree in the Faculty of Sciences. How I admired her! How I envied her! Laura was on cloud nine.

I'd begun studying calculus at a private university. But I thought it was really bad. I was planning to transfer into Mathematics at the University of Buenos Aires. I didn't really know why I'd ended up at that private university. Probably because Raúl was studying psychology there, as well as my fear of the entrance exam for the national one.

Dad was really happy about my decision to study math. I was thrilled that Dad was enthusiastic about something to do with me. I felt like we shared a secret by being interested in science. Just the two of us. Dad was an astrophysicist. He'd been a full professor of Physics from '59 to '66. When I told him I was going into the Faculty of Science, he was alarmed. We were still under the military dictatorship. Dad was frightened that there would still be professors from back then who'd been ideologically opposed to him and would treat me badly for being his daughter. Dad had been thrown out during the night of the long knives. I'd heard it hundreds of times, never in detail, but I knew Dad had been very distressed.

Laura talked nonstop about the guys in her faculty. She thought they were fascinating. They talked about politics and worried about the country. Some of them rented apartments and lived on their own or with friends. They had study groups. According to Laura, they all knew my surname: "The Goldmans are famous in the Science Faculty, they're idols." There wasn't a single person she met in the faculty who hadn't heard of my family. I felt really proud. It reminded me of my childhood. It reminded me of when Dad had taken care of me. I was too little when Dad was a university professor but I well remembered the years he'd been director of the Radio Astronomy Institute. The Institute was in Pereyra Iraola Park. Dad took us there every weekend. I loved Dad a lot. So many years had gone by since then! Just to think, Dad didn't even know Susana yet. How wonderful!

Laura had crushes on several guys in the faculty. All older than her. Some of them were TAs. But there was one she liked especially called Enrique. Laura had nicknamed him Quique. Quique was in his fourth year of a Physics degree, he was left-wing and a great admirer of my dad. He'd started college the year of the Soccer World Cup.

One Saturday afternoon, Quique was going over to Laura's house. It was my chance to meet him. I was still going out with Raúl. After the incident with the cops, Raúl got really scared and had been staying straight. Quique, Laura, Raúl and I spent the whole afternoon talking. Quique told us exciting stories about university politics. We were in the middle of the Malvinas War over those islands the English called the Falklands. Quique thought the university cops were at a loss as to how to react. "Guys from the Communist Party stand up to give speeches in the bar and when the cops are about to grab them, they come out in favor of the war against the English in the Malvinas Islands; then the cops back off."

That whole world seemed wonderful to me. It reminded me of Dad when I was a kid. He was left-wing too, when he taught in the Science Faculty. I wanted to get into that faculty as soon as possible. Quique spoke really highly of my dad, even though he hadn't known him personally. I was ashamed to tell him my dad wasn't involved in physics anymore and directed a project for a bunch of Argentinian investors in New York.

Quique and Laura saw quite a bit of each other, but just to sleep together. I knew Laura, although she never said so, really wanted to be Quique's girlfriend. I could see it saddened her that Quique only went out with her so he could fuck her.

One day, Quique phoned Laura's place. I answered. We chatted for a while. I told him I had a math exam coming up. He offered to help me. We agreed he'd come over to my place to explain functions and relations to me.

Quique came over on a Saturday afternoon. He explained some math to me. I was happy to know someone normal. After it got dark, I mentioned that Raúl hadn't called me all day. When he was leaving, he said next time my boyfriend wasn't taking me out on a Saturday night, he'd ask me out. I didn't answer.

A few days later, Dad came to Buenos Aires. Since all Susana's kids lived in New York by then, she didn't come anymore. Dad came on his own. Dad said he hated Argentina. That his only reason for coming was to see me. Dad stayed at the Plaza. We spent hours talking in his room, we went out for meals and walks.

When Daddy came to Buenos Aires, I felt protected. During those days I didn't have to worry about myself. I put off any troubles until after Dad left. I felt like while he was there, nothing bad could happen to me.

That year Dad had started sending me tons of money each month. I could save some. Ana, a friend from the university, told me that apartments were really cheap. I suggested to Daddy that we buy a studio apartment. I could contribute my savings. I dreamed of having my own place. Four days later, Dad paid the reserve deposit for an apartment in Palermo Chico. I couldn't quite believe it. Dad had never bought me anything so expensive. My savings had covered the down payment.

I told Daddy that Laura was studying Physics in the Faculty of Sciences. "All the guys in the faculty know who you are and admire you a lot," I told him. Quique wanted to interview Daddy for the faculty magazine. Dad loved the idea, but in the end there wasn't time.

The day after he left, I phoned Quique. We talked for ages. He asked if I wanted to come over to his house. I knew Quique lived alone. Before I hung up, he asked, "Are you sure you know what you're doing?" I answered yes. The phone rang as soon as I hung it up: it was Raúl. He was furious. He shouted that he'd been trying to call me all day and hadn't been able to get through. I didn't care. I told him that it was already late and we should see each other the next day.

Quique lived in San Telmo. It was already dark when I left home. It was really cold. I took a taxi. I couldn't stop shivering. I felt like everything was really weird. I didn't know what was going on. I was happy thinking that, for the first time, I could talk to a guy who had something going on upstairs. I imagined we'd talk about the plague of generals we'd had in government for the last six years and that idiot, Galtieri, who'd got us into the Malvinas War.

We sat on opposite sides of his desk. Suddenly, he asked if he could kiss me. He took me completely by surprise. I didn't know what to answer but I said no. He was surprised too. I began to realize what a mess I'd gotten myself into.

I didn't suppose he'd believe me if I tried to explain that I'd only come to his house to talk, not to make love. I didn't dare tell him. Quique thought it was incredible I didn't want him to kiss me. "Would you mind telling me what the hell you were thinking when I asked if you were sure you knew what you were doing?" I didn't know what to tell him. "I knew Quique lived on his own... I like him, he likes me... But I can't screw around on Laura like this ... and Raúl.... Laura was in love with Quique.... Shit, what a fuck-up!" I thought. "I can't screw around on Laura," I said. "Screw around on Laura? Is that what you're worried about now? But don't you realize you screwed Laura just by coming here? Whether we fuck or not, nothing's going to change that," said Quique.

I'd never fooled around on Raúl. Anyway, Laura mattered more to me than Raúl. "If I do it, I'll kill two birds with one stone," I thought. Quique tried to convince me to make love. I didn't know how to manage the situation. It was the first time I'd been in something like this with a guy I respected. I didn't know what excuse to give him anymore.

Suddenly, Quique felt bad. He said I'd done it on purpose. He started telling me about his father, who died when he was little, and his stepfather, who was really ill. "I would never have done this to you on purpose. How can you think that?" He seemed to believe me. "Lucky for you I'm a nice guy," said Quique, "you're not in danger with me. But be careful, babe, because you do this to another guy and they'll knock the shit out of you and fuck you right there." I managed a frightened smile.

We said good night at about three in the morning. When I was about to get on the elevator, he said to me from the door, "Luz, one thing I can tell you for sure, this isn't over."

Although I didn't want to accept it, I imagined what Quique said would be true: we'd meet again. On the one hand, I was ashamed of what I'd done, but on the other, I thought I'd behaved decently by not sleeping with Quique.

From that moment on, I started to feel more sure of myself. Raúl mattered less and less to me and I realized that other guys were interested in me. I knew I wouldn't go out with druggies anymore. I changed my way of dressing. For the last few years I'd been dressing like a lady, I looked like Raúl's mother. I started wearing miniskirts, jeans and sneakers; being more comfortable.

A few days later, once again, I had a big argument with Raúl. It was Friday. We decided not to see each other that night. Much to my surprise, it didn't worry me.

I phoned Quique. I told him I'd had a fight with Raúl. "Come over, if you want," he said.

Again I found myself in a taxi on my way to Quique's. This time we didn't talk much. It had all been said already and we fucked straightaway. I didn't find Quique as attractive as I would have liked, but I loved being able to talk about politics with him in bed.

The next morning Raúl phoned. He spent ages telling me what he'd done the night before. I didn't pay attention. He asked me what I'd done. "I stayed home."

After hanging up, I burst into tears. I bawled my eyes out. I knew I wasn't interested in Raúl at all anymore. But even so, I didn't have the courage to break up with him.

XVI

I had to take a make-up exam in Mathematics. I decided to call Juan to get some tutoring. Juan was a Mathematics student in the Science Faculty. Juan remembered me and seemed enthusiastic at my proposal.

As soon as Juan arrived, I told him I had a friend majoring in Physics and that I was planning to start in Mathematics the following year. The Malvinas War had just ended. We talked a lot about that. I mentioned to Juan that from the beginning I supposed England would win and I thought that would be good. He laughed. He recommended I be careful not to go around telling that to just anyone. I was embarrassed. I explained that it wasn't that I actually preferred a victory for England, but that I was sure, in the case of Argentina winning, we'd never ever get the generals off our backs. Juan agreed with me on that.

I felt attracted to Juan that day.

The afternoon before my exam, I had my last class with Juan. I wasn't going to see him again. Before we finished, he mentioned that a friend of his was going to New York and would be seeing my dad. If I wanted to send a letter or something, all I had to do was ask. I said yes, I'd very much like to send something.

For a while I did nothing but think about Juan. Maybe he liked me too. "Well, after all, every time he comes to the house he stays for ages after class to talk." And, there was the offer from his friend. But I couldn't really convince myself. I didn't know what to think. It seemed impossible that Juan would take any notice of me. I tried to calculate how old he was. He'd gone to Nacional Buenos Aires, which meant he'd done six years of high school instead of five. Then he'd started Med School, that was another year. Then he studied

Chemistry for three years, and for at least the last three he'd been doing Mathematics. He must be about twenty-five. And I was eighteen!

I told Laura I had a huge crush on Juan and didn't know what to do.

I phoned Juan a few days before his friend was leaving for New York. I had a letter ready for Dad, a present for my brother Luis and a carton of Parisienne cigarettes for Pablo.

Juan and his friend came over. Through the intercom I heard: "It's Juan, your math teacher." The three of us chatted for a bit. I mentioned to Juan that I'd split up with Raúl, which had nothing to do with anything and furthermore was a lie. Juan stood there the whole time and refused to sit down. I realized he was terribly shy and the only way anything could happen between us was if it was perfectly obvious that I wasn't going out with Raúl anymore. And anyway, getting involved with the ex-girlfriend of his young student wasn't going to leave him with a very clear conscience.

The three of us left together. At the comer I told them I was going to the apartment my dad had bought me. I was going to try to install some light bulb sockets. Raúl was going too, but I didn't happen to mention that fact. Juan told me if I ever needed any help installing lights or anything, to let him know; he knew a thing or two about electricity. I felt very excited. I said I would definitely call him.

That weekend I was with Raúl. I couldn't take him anymore. I could not stand him. I just couldn't bear his presence or the way he was. Monday night he called me. He was really angry. What was this, not phoning him all day? "I'm sick, I spent the day in bed. How come you didn't come to see me? You're such a bitch!" He talked and talked. He insulted me. Told me I was a piece of shit. The usual. But this time, after almost four years, nothing he said mattered to me. I didn't try to convince him I wasn't a shit. I didn't say a word. I hung up. I was surprised at myself. I'd never felt like that before.

The next day I went out for lunch with Mara. I told her about my feelings for Juan. That the only way to see him was to phone him and I was really embarrassed to do it. She insisted I should phone him: "Nothing ventured, nothing gained, Luz." I'd never ventured anything.

Without another thought, I phoned Juan as soon as I got back home. He answered. I told him that the Saturday before I hadn't put the bulb sockets in and that, well, since he'd offered to help me... He reiterated that, of course, he'd be glad to. I asked him when might be convenient. "I could make it this afternoon." We arranged to meet at the apartment. I had the sockets but when I got there I realized we weren't going to be able to install them: the building was new and they hadn't connected the electricity to my apartment yet.

I bumped into Juan at the entrance. I'd arrived before, and just when I went down to look for the doorman, we met. I pretended I just got there.

There wasn't a single piece of furniture. Juan liked the apartment. He told me his mother had a very similar one. At one point he'd thought of moving in, but in the end he hadn't and his mother had rented it out. I described the alterations I was planning to make and showed him where I was going to put the dividing wall. While we walked around I could feel him watching me. I just kept talking. I had a miniskirt on. I noticed Juan didn't take his eyes off me.

We sat on the floor leaning against one of the walls. I told him about my cousin who'd been disappeared and his sister who'd been run over by a car and killed when she was eight months pregnant. I felt strange going over my past. I never did that. Raúl wasn't interested. The only thing he ever said to me, on those occasions, was that I shouldn't give a shit about my parents because when I was little they hadn't given a fuck about me.

Juan told me about his high school years. He'd been in sixth year in '73, the year Perón came back from exile. He wasn't a member of any political party but sympathized with the *per-*

onistas. My aunt Elena had been a *peronista* too. Juan made me think of my childhood, when I still believed in something. The years when my family was still together. We realized that some classmates of his from high school were the daughters of an ex-girlfriend of Dad's. Afterwards, I didn't see them again. One of them was called Luz. She was six years older than me. I had bad memories of Luz: she never lent me her dolls, they were on a shelf and she wouldn't let me touch them.

Juan and I talked for ages. Being alone with him was marvellous. Raúl had a key to the apartment. I was afraid he'd come in.

It started to get dark. There were no lights. No candles either. Juan's features were getting steadily blurrier. I was enjoying the possibility of sensing the growing darkness. They hadn't connected the telephone either. We were completely isolated. Suddenly, we looked at each other. The conversation seemed to have come to an end. But it was just a look; we kept talking about something else.

A bit of light from next door came in through the window. Juan held my hand. I caressed his. We kissed. I liked it. I felt really attracted to Juan. For the first time, I felt really turned on by a man. I couldn't bring myself to touch him too much. He did though, Juan was gentle. He was a real man. But I said, "No, not today." It was nighttime. We could barely see each other. We didn't know what to say. Suddenly, I thought I should be getting home. They hadn't heard a thing from me since this morning.

Juan walked me to the bus stop. He said he felt a bit guilty for having seduced his young student's girlfriend, not to mention hitting on his own student. We laughed. We left it that we'd speak on the phone the next day.

XVII

I met Juan the next night. He came straight from teaching a class. Juan lived in Parque Patricios. I'd never been there.

I was surprised that anyone should live in that area. My friends were from Barrio Norte, Palermo Chico or Belgrano, no further.

We went for a coffee and then to the apartment. We continued talking there by candlelight. Juan said he had something for me. "I brought you a present." I couldn't believe it and got embarrassed. I didn't know what to say. Juan made light of it. He kissed me and started to caress me. Nevertheless, he noticed I wasn't ready. "I really want to make love to you, but if you don't want to, that's okay." When we were on the landing I noticed I hadn't even taken my coat off and it was much earlier than I thought I'd seen on my watch.

Walking down the street, I told him my dad sent me fifteen hundred dollars a month, three hundred of which I gave to Mom for my expenses. At the beginning of each month I went to a bank to pick up the money. He was laughing at me as I told him. I felt a mixture of pride and shame. I knew it was a huge amount of money. Juan calculated that I received more money than a government minister. Not bad for a daughter's salary. I told him that up till then my dad had never sent me that much money. Juan was struck. I suddenly feared he would want me for my money and regretted having told him.

That night Juan told me he was going out with someone but they weren't a couple and he didn't like her all that much. He didn't really see much future in that relationship. I still hadn't even broken off with Raúl and at that moment, I was relieved I hadn't.

We arranged to meet two days later in Salguero again. I went to buy a double mattress in the morning. They delivered it a little while before Juan arrived. He helped me get it into place and then we made love. I felt really turned on by Juan, making love with him was completely different to everything I'd known up until then. Juan was attentive. He told me I was beautiful. He cared about me feeling pleasure. I'd never experienced anything like it. I felt, for the first time, what it was like to be treated well by a man in bed. I mattered to him.

I loved Juan's body. I noticed he liked mine a lot too. Juan had a virile body. He wasn't hairless like Raúl. I felt proud of making love with him.

We were together all afternoon and then Juan went to teach a class. Before leaving, he put on a pair of glasses. I didn't think they suited him. He said he wore them to look more like a prof.

I didn't see Raúl for several days. Now I had to talk to him urgently, tell him I didn't want to be his girlfriend anymore. Still, I was scared of regretting it. Partly because Juan was still seeing the other girl. Partly because I knew I'd have to face tons of my own problems covered up by our relationship. I had a feeling that when we talked, Raúl was going to get really angry with me and maybe even hit me.

Juan and I always got together in Salguero. It was our place. I never went to that apartment alone. I'd arrive a few minutes before Juan and we'd go up together. Sometimes, Ester would ask me where I'd been all afternoon. Mom never asked me anything. I couldn't bring myself to tell her I went to Salguero.

One Sunday night I came home after being with Juan all day. Mom told me Raúl had called several times and had even come by looking for me. Mom got mad at me. She said if I didn't want to go out with Raúl anymore I should speak to him as soon as possible and give him an explanation.

Two days later the situation had reached the breaking point. Raúl was phoning me constantly. I'd run out of excuses.

But I couldn't bring myself to just come right out and tell him I didn't want to see him anymore either.

I phoned him. I'd made up my mind to break up with him no matter what, and I went over to his house.

I found him shut up in his smoke-filled room as usual. It was a large bedroom. Beside the bed was a television and behind it the bathroom door. He turned on the TV every time I tried to say something. He wouldn't let go of the remote. Raúl's family couldn't live without television: there was one in every room. The phone was also within arm's reach. They all communicated by telephone. When Raúl's parents wanted to tell him something, they phoned him, even though their room was next to his. For Raúl's dad to come into his room was an event. In the drawers of the dresser alongside his bed, Raúl kept pot, a little box of joints, cocaine wrapped in tin foil and, sometimes, syringes. On top of that dresser was his stereo and the lamp: To cover up all the smells, Raúl wore tons of cologne. Raúl's cologne disgusted me. It made him seem like a fag. In spite of everything, I still loved him a little and I felt like talking to him.

Raúl greeted me coldly, as if he hadn't been demanding to see me. He asked me what I'd been up to the last few days. He had a blank expression on his face. I told him I'd reached the conclusion that things between the two of us just couldn't go on anymore. But I felt like talking to him, I thought we could help each other. I talked and talked for a while and Raúl didn't say a single word. I had the feeling he wasn't even listening to me. It couldn't be that he had nothing at all to say on the subject. When I couldn't think of anything more to tell him, I asked what he was thinking. "I've got nothing to say to you," he replied.

I didn't know what to do. We said goodbye as if nothing had happened. I left his house completely confused. Raúl didn't yell at me, he didn't hit me, he didn't speak to me. He'd said, "I've got nothing to say to you," and turned on the television.

XVIII

Dad had told me he'd be coming to Buenos Aires in November. He wanted us to celebrate my birthday together but, in the end, he couldn't make it. He was too busy with work. So I told him never to promise me he was going to come and visit until he was sure he'd be able to. So many times he'd told me he was coming to see me and then, at the last minute, something would come up!

Dad phoned me in December. He told me he really wanted to see me so why didn't I book a ticket for Río de Janeiro, for that very Friday, and he'd meet me there on Saturday morning. "At nine, in the Hotel Sol Ipanema." We'd spend three days together. Just the two of us.

I told Mom I was going and her face contracted sourly as was to be expected. But I didn't care anymore.

Friday night I took the plane to Río. I arrived at the hotel and asked for the reservation under the name of Goldman. It was there. There were two rooms reserved for that name. I was thrilled to verify that Dad had taken care of everything.

It reminded me of the dad I'd had when I was little: the dad that was always on top of everything. If Dad showed me the way, I could feel safe in any part of the world.

I woke up early. I went across to the beach. At nine I went back to the hotel. Dad was just coming in. How marvellous! Dad, on time! He had assured me he'd arrive at that time and here he was. I felt that, once again, I could trust Dad. We greeted each other smiling. We were happy to see each other again.

We went to the beach together. For me, it was an unusual situation. We'd never been on our own, just the two of us. I told Dad I was seeing Juan. Dad was pleased he was a Mathematics student. He asked me if he would specialize in "pure" or "applied." I didn't know but I answered that he'd specialize in "pure." "They're too dreamy," said Dad. Dad liked me reminding him of his time on the Faculty of Sciences. When he talked about those years his whole expression changed, he spoke with love and pride. Having approached that world, I felt like Dad and I could share something very private. Neither Luis nor any of Susana's kids had pursued a scientific education. I seemed to be the only one who could appreciate this side of Dad.

In the evening, we went out for a walk. Dad looked at me and said I was pretty. I got embarrassed. I asked him if it mattered whether his students were pretty or not when he was a professor. He said yes. "All teachers notice if their students are pretty."

That day Dad gave me my birthday present: earrings and a necklace he'd brought me from Egypt. I loved them. Only then did I feel like I'd really had my birthday. No one gave me gifts as nice as Dad's.

We arranged to meet the next morning on the top floor of the hotel for breakfast. When we went to the beach we started to talk about ourselves. I told him I'd always felt bad at his house. I criticized Susana. Dad got angry. He forbade me to speak harshly about a woman he'd fallen in love with. I felt hurt, unimportant, but I pretended not to care. "Since you and Susana got married, you've treated Luis, Susana's kids and me like we were all brothers and sisters; Susana, on the other hand, has always put Luis and me down." Dad said it wasn't true, that he put money away for Luis's and my future but not for Susana's kids. "It's true that if I separated from Susana, I would eventually see her kids and I suppose she wouldn't see you two." "If I separated from Susana..." It seemed strange to hear this from Dad. Dad had never said such a thing... "And besides, I can barely tolerate José anymore," Dad added. "Susana and I have agreed that if he gets thrown out of school one more time, we're sending him to a boarding school. I don't want to see him in the house anymore, I'm completely fed up with him." Poor Dad! I thought. He'd expended so much energy bringing up Susana's kids and now they were all nuts; they brought him nothing but trouble. What a drag!

Then I told him about Inés. I said I hated her. "However, she's always envied you. You've got a dad who loves you and cares about you; Inés doesn't." It would never in a million years have occurred to me that Inés could possibly be jealous of me.

We also talked about the work he was doing then. He told me he couldn't stand it anymore. He was exhausted. He didn't get any time to himself. His dream was to get back into writing. After writing two text books on astronomy and a popularizing one called *The Origin of the Stars*, he hadn't published anything else. And it had been eleven years now.

Dad told me he wanted to get back into astronomy. I felt really excited, I could have kissed him, hugged him. Daddy! "So, why don't you?" "Well, it would be a bit difficult taking it up again, I'm way behind the times. Besides, there's the financial side. If I go back to scientific research, I'll never make enough to support everyone." "But I don't care, send me less money, it's no problem for me." Dad, an astronomer again! I thought. And separated from Susana! It was my ideal... "Well, I'll tell you, I have been talking to some researchers at Harvard, people from my day. I'm starting to get some contacts again." I couldn't believe my ears. I wanted to study mathematics and knew how important science could be in a person's life. That's what Dad was. Dad was an astronomer. "Luz, I want you to tell me everything you're feeling, that way I can be a better dad." I'd never felt so moved by anything Dad had ever said to me. I felt he was being sincere, that he was saying it with love. I didn't know how to answer him. I smiled.

In the afternoon, after a shower, I went to Dad's room. We sat and talked. There was less than a year to go until the 1983 national elections. I was interested to know what he thought about it. "Who'd you vote for in '73?" He'd voted for Coral: "There were a few worthwhile people in his party. In '74, I voted for Alende." I remembered that. "Right now I think the only decent politician in Argentina is Alfonsín." But Dad had little hope for the political future of Argentina. "They'll leave power in civilian hands for the moment because the country's broke, but as soon as the cow gets fattened up again, they'll stage another coup. Though with the size of the foreign debt, I think it'll be quite a few years before there's anything in the treasury." I tried not to take too much notice of his pessimistic remarks. I'd never talked about politics with Dad even though he'd been personally affected by the changes of government in Argentina. His nephew had been disappeared for five years and Dad was still searching for information on his whereabouts. For Dad, Marcos's disappearance was unforgivable.

Those days in Río de Janeiro seemed like a dream to me. One night we went to the cinema. Then we went for a drink at the Garota de Ipanema. The movie was about a troubled relationship between a father and son. They were Russian immigrants in the United States. In the last scene, the father and son hug tightly. An embrace of reconciliation. Dad looked sad on the way out of the cinema. We walked for a bit. Dad kept silent. "I'll never get over my dad dying and not having been able to hug him, no last embrace," said Dad, with tears in his eyes but without actually crying.

That night we kept talking in the hotel foyer. I talked to Dad about things I'd never been able to tell him. About his marriage to Susana, his desertion of us, the pain of watching him taking care of someone else's kids and not us anymore. I had a lump in my throat. My voice faltered. I tried to cover up my pain. I didn't dare cry.

The next day was Sunday. There was a handicrafts fair on. I suggested we go. He agreed. "He really seems like a changed man," I thought. "Dad, wasting a whole afternoon at a crafts fair?" He seemed happy. He bought me a handbag and a pair of sandals. I didn't even have to ask. He bought me some clothes too. I told Dad I was going to take a present back for Mom. Dad picked out a blouse for her. "Dad buying a blouse for Mom? What was this?" I was really pleased I'd be able to tell Mom that Dad had chosen her present.

Monday night my visit with Dad came to an end. I packed slowly. I put my new clothes in the suitcase. Dad and I met in the lobby. We took a taxi to the airport. We were really tanned. We'd had beautiful sunny weather every day. We talked about what a great time we'd had. I asked Dad if he'd ever been to Salvador. "No, never." I suggested next time we meet there. He thought it was a great idea. Dad loved travelling. At that moment, so did I. I imagined wonderful trips with Dad. My plane left first. I'd get into Buenos Aires at midnight. It would still be summer. Dad would land in New York the next morning. It was winter there.

Airports had always made me sad. The everlasting separations. That last moment when no one knew what to say. And once again, the feeling of powerlessness I got from having to live so far away from people I loved. In any case, that time I felt closer to Dad than I ever had. It seemed to me that parting was a little less sad. Dad asked me to write to him and not to hesitate to tell him everything I was going through.

We said goodbye before I went into the departure lounge. "Well, Luz, I hope this time it really will be 'see you soon.'"

"Yeah, Daddy, for sure; I've got my entrance exam in March and then I'm on vacation until classes start. I can come and see you." "Maybe we could meet in Europe," he replied. "I've got to go to Greece some time around then." "O.K. Dad, well, we'll definitely be seeing each other, wherever." We hugged and, without another word, looked at each other for the last time.

About the Author and the Book

Paula Varsavsky is a journalist, novelist and short story writer. She is the author of two novels, *Nadie alzaba la voz* (Emecé, 1994) and *El resto de su vida* (Mondadori, 2007), both of which are taught at several universities in Argentina, the United States, and Germany. *Nadie alzaba la voz* was translated into English by Anne McLean as *No One Said a Word* and first published in hardcover by Ontario Review Press (2000).

She is also the author of a collection of short stories, *El retrato* (soon to be published by Editorial Alfaguara). Her short stories have been published in journals and anthologies, such as *Lamujerdemivida, Translation, World Literature Today, Hostos Review, Revista Cultural Avatares* and *In Our Own Words: A Generation Defining Itself*. Currently, she is working on her third novel to be published under the title *Una clásica historia de política y poder*.

Varsavsky is the daughter of noted Argentinian astrophysicist, Dr. Carlos Vasavsky. After the murder of a family member during the "Dirty Wars" in Argentina, the Varsavsky family moved to New York in 1977. *No One Said a Word* is set during this same time period, but feels almost apolitical, accurately reflecting the vacuous lives of its affluent adolescent narrator and her peers. Critics have called *No One Said a Word* "the Argentinian *Catcher in the Rye*."

About the Translator

Anne McLean is a Canadian translator who lives and translates in Yorkshire. She holds a MA in Literary Translation and has translated works by Julio Cortázar, Javier Cercas, Evelio Rosero, among others. She was awarded the Independent Foreign Fiction Prize in 2009 and 2004 for her translations of *Los ejércitos* and *Soldados de Salamina*.

Acknowledgments

Many people lent a hand during the writing, translating and publishing of this book in varied and unforgettable ways. My heartfelt thanks to: Santiago Kovadloff, my creative writing professor, for his constant encouragement, patience and meticulous reading of the original, Lea Fletcher, Elena Castedo, Bonifacio del Carril and Mercedes Güiraldes for the Spanish edition, David and Jean Layzer, Gene Bell-Villada, Josefina Ludmer, Anne McLean for her sensitivity with the translation, Marion Winik, Martín Varsavsky and Francisco Goldman.

My thanks also to Francisco Lala, my beloved son, and to Raymond Smith and Joyce Carol Oates, for their belief in this book.

Wings Press was founded in 1975 by Joanie Whitebird and Joseph F. Lomax, both deceased. Bryce Milligan has been the publisher, editor and designer since 1995. The mission of Wings Press is to publish the finest in American writing—meaning all of the Americas—without commercial considerations clouding the choice to publish or not to publish. Technically a "for profit" press, Wings receives only occasional underwriting from individuals and institutions who wish to support our vision. For this we are very grateful.

Wings Press attempts to produce multicultural books, chapbooks, ebooks, and broadsides that enlighten the human spirit and enliven the mind. Everyone ever associated with Wings has been or is a writer, and we know well that writing is a transformational art form capable of changing the world, primarily by allowing us to glimpse something of each other's souls. Good writing is innovative, insightful, and interesting. But most of all it is honest.

Likewise, Wings Press is committed to treating the planet itself as a partner. Thus the press uses soy and other vegetable-based inks, and as much recycled material as possible, from the paper on which the books are printed to the boxes in which they are shipped.

As Robert Dana wrote in *Against the Grain*, "Small press publishing is personal publishing. In essence, it's a matter of personal vision, personal taste and courage, and personal friendships." Welcome to our world.

Colophon

This paperback edition of *No One Said a Word,* by Paula Varsavsky, has been printed on 55 pound EB "natural" paper containing a high percentage of recycled fiber. Titles have been set in Chalkduster type, the text in Adobe Caslon type. All Wings Press books are designed and produced by Bryce Milligan.

On-line catalogue and ordering available at
www.wingspress.com

Wings Press titles are distributed to the trade by the
Independent Publishers Group
www.ipgbook.com
and in Europe by
www.gazellebookservices.co.uk

Also available as an ebook.